The Last Giant

Also by Mario Milosevic

Terrastina and Mazolli: a Novel in 99-word Episodes
Animal Life
Fantasy Life
Love Life

The Last Giant

Mario Milosevic

Ruby Rose's Fairy Tale Emporium • 2011

The Last Giant
by Mario Milosevic

Copyright © 2011 by Mario Milosevic

ISBN-13: 978-1456507428
ISBN-10: 1456507427

All rights reserved.

No part of this book may be reproduced without written permission of the author.

A production of
Ruby Rose's Fairy Tale Emporium
Published by Green Snake Publishing
www.greensnakepublishing.com

mariowrites.com

For Dave

firefly

Firefly's stick chair clattered sharply against the wooden floor of her tiny house. Her bowl of venison stew vibrated on the wooden table in front of her. Firefly's mother, seated next to her, ate stew from her own bowl.

They both looked up at the ceiling of beams that had been cut from trees harvested by giants. Dust shook loose from the beams and began sifting through the air in pale clouds.

Firefly's chair clattered again. Her spoon knocked against her bowl. "That's a giant," she said, "come down for a tattoo."

Firefly lived with her mother on the placid big river in Craddleton, a tiny village of several dozen small houses. Craddleton, like the other villages in the gorge, clung to the bank of the river and was shadowed by towering cliff walls that rose hundreds of feet to a plateau above them, which was where the giants lived and worked.

For as long as Firefly could remember, tremors from the ground had regularly rattled the gorge, making trees tremble and houses shake. Such shaking and trembling was an accepted consequence of living below a realm populated by giants. Everyone was used to the quakes and everyone knew where they came from.

For the past few weeks, however, many more quakes than normal had been shaking the villages. To Firefly, and to most other river people, the tremors had a different feel from the usual vibrations in the ground. They lasted longer. They lodged in the pit of the stomach. They made everyone's heart beat faster. The tremors felt like they came not from giants treading on the plateau, but from somewhere deeper, perhaps from the ground itself.

But on this morning, when the ground rumbled and quaked, the source was unmistakable.

"Mom," said Firefly, "I want to go with you and help you do the tattoo."

"Ink with me?" said her mother. "Don't be silly."

Firefly's mother never wanted her to join the family trade, but from the time Firefly was old enough to crawl, right up to the present day, which was only a couple of months after her fourteenth birthday, all Firefly wanted was to tattoo the giants. She'd seen them, and she felt their footsteps in the ground as they walked. The whole earth trembled whenever the giants came down from the plateau and waited at the foot of the cliffs for the river people to attend to them.

Firefly stood up, barely able to contain her excitement. "Why can't I go with you?" she said. She had asked this question many times and always received the same answer. Which never stopped her from asking it again.

"It's hard work for little reward," said her mother. She put on her heavy work clothes and slipped the harness, which held the vats of ink, onto her shoulders. Firefly watched her prepare, mesmerized. She wanted nothing more than to be an inker like her mother. She adored the whole process: the drawing, the inking, the climbing up on the giant.

"I have all these ideas for tattoos," said Firefly. "I want to do one of the ice dam, and another one of a giant's cave, and one of the place where they build their circles. I think the giants would like them."

"I'm sure," said her mother. "But Firefly, you are much too young to be doing something so dangerous. And anyway, I have never seen inking as your destiny."

Firefly's shoulders slumped. "But that's what I want," she said.

Her mother put down her needle, a foot long wooden tube with a sharp point on the tip. The other end of the needle trailed hoses made of hollow plant stems attached to nozzles on the ink canisters. "You are too impulsive," said her mother. "Inking requires careful planning and execution. That is not your strong suit, I'm afraid. You are always deciding you need to go on an adventure."

"Adventures are fun," said Firefly.

"Yes, but even the best inker can be hurt easily and you, Firefly, with your careless ways would be in even worse danger. You must understand, Firefly, inking is a dying art. The giants don't want tattoos like they used to. It's best for you never to get the taste of the craft. If you decide to be an inker when you are of age, there is nothing I can do about it. Until then I am going to do my best to steer you otherwise. Now let's get you to Mr. Epiderm's house. You need to attend to your studies."

Firefly finished the last of her stew and followed her mother out the door. A tiny sliver of the sun peeked over the cliff walls as they walked quickly along a road that was little more than a narrow path between the tiny houses of Firefly's fellow Craddletonians. The air was cold, but Firefly did not mind. She liked being outside with her inker mother. She liked listening to the bird songs that filled the space between the cliff walls. It was like the songs were filling her heart. She loved the smell of new spring flowers and the taste of something new in the air. She liked the way other people looked at them. Her mother did an important and dangerous job. People respected that.

They stopped near Mr. Epiderm's house. "I'm going to go on to the clearing now," said Firefly's mother. "You make sure you go directly to Mr. Epiderm's. I don't want you wandering off on any of your adventures. Do you understand?"

Firefly nodded. "Yes, Mom," she said.

"Promise?"

"Promise."

"Good." Firefly's mother kissed her on the forehead and turned and walked toward the cliff face where a sandy clearing big enough for the giants awaited her. Firefly looked up to the edge of the cliff where the giants lived. Sometimes she saw them walking along the tree line. And sometimes the giants stopped and looked down at the river. She loved knowing they lived above her, protecting the river people from danger.

And her mother, her own mother, got to ink them. She sighed and stood staring for a few seconds, then turned and resumed walking down the street. She passed the community cooking pit where the cooks were busy setting up a spit for roasting a deer that one of the giants had brought down for them. The cooks waved at her. "Time for your lessons Firefly?" they called.

Firefly nodded and waved back and pointed at the spit." Looks like we'll be having a good dinner tonight," she said.

"Thanks to the giants," they said.

Firefly walked by a pile of deer skins. They smelled so rich she wanted to stand in their aroma and inhale for hours. The skins would be scraped and tanned and floated to Waffleton on rowboats where expert sewers would make them into shirts and pants for the giants. Everyone helped everyone else in the gorge and on the plateau.

She arrived at wrinkled old Mr. Epiderm's wooden house. She knocked on the door. "Come in, Firefly," came Mr. Epiderm's voice.

Firefly pushed the door open and stepped into the house. "My mother doesn't want me to be an inker," she said.

Mr. Epiderm looked up from his stick chair and raised his bushy white eyebrows at her. "Indeed," he said.

"Yeah," said Firefly. "It isn't fair."

"I'm sorry, Firefly," he said. "I know you want to be an inker, but your mother knows best, don't you think?"

Firefly nodded. "I suppose so." She sat in her

chair across from her tutor. Mr. Epiderm needed two canes to help himself get around. He used to be an inker way back before Firefly was born, even before her parents had been born. He had to give up the trade when one of the giants sneezed during an inking. Mr. Epiderm fell off the giant's shoulder and hit the ground very hard, breaking a knee. Which was bad enough, but then the giant rolled over and crushed Mr. Epiderm's legs, breaking them in many places. The healers did the best they could to mend his injuries, but he was never the same. He could not climb up the ladders and scamper about on the giants, which was necessary to practice his trade. Since he wasn't any good for much besides sitting in chairs after that, Mr. Epiderm became a scholar. He was well known as a very good tutor, and not only in Craddleton. Everyone on the big river respected his knowledge and character. He spent most of his days making paper from the reeds gathered for him by the children of the gorge. He wrote on the pages, filling them with his scribbles and stories that no one ever read. The rest of the time he tutored young students like Firefly. Her mother said they were very lucky to have him as a guide for Firefly's studies.

Firefly was sure Mr. Epiderm was at least a hundred years old. Maybe two.

Mr. Epiderm began their lesson by singing an

old song Firefly knew by heart:

> In morning light,
> my heart's delight,
>
> is slinking in
> and inking skin.
>
> To draw the fire
> of your heart's desire;
>
> to break your bones
> and hear your moans.

Firefly's mother taught this song to her when she was a baby. Firefly began singing it almost from the day she could talk. Mr. Epiderm's rendition of it today was strong and loud. No one would think, after hearing his full voice sing the song, that he was any kind of weakling. The song almost always cheered Firefly up. Not this time, though. Mr. Epiderm sang it two more times. "I see I must find a different approach," he said.

"What do you mean?" said Firefly.

"I have never seen you so morose," said Mr. Epiderm. "I think perhaps I need to give you some math problems to cheer you up. No learning can happen if you have a heavy heart."

Not even a good round of story problems could cheer her up this time, thought Firefly. But Mr. Epiderm insisted. He pulled out a sheet of problems involving the weight of rock a giant could carry, the number of heartbeats a creature might have in a year, the force that various water wheels could produce under varying rates of flow, and the cooking times of several weights of animals on rotating spits over open fires. Despite her mood, Firefly fell on the problems eagerly, filling up the sheet with calculations and equations. When she was finished she handed the paper to Mr. Epiderm who studied it carefully and soon declared Firefly's answers flawless. "Very good work," he said. "And now do you feel better? Are you ready for some history lessons?"

Firefly did feel better, although she still could not rid herself of the thought that inking was her true calling. "Mr. Epiderm," she said, "the way things are going now, it looks like I will never be an inker. What should I do?"

Mr. Epiderm looked as though he was considering the question very carefully. He held up his hands and signed some words. *We need to switch to signing, now. We don't want to get out of practice.*

Firefly held up her hands. *OK.* It was fine with Firefly. She liked signing and Mr. Epiderm always said she was a fine signer, one of his quickest students.

My job is not to give you advice, he signed. *It is to teach you what you need to know.*

That's just it, signed Firefly. *What* do *I need to know? If I can't ink I don't want to do anything else. I think when I get old enough, I must leave Craddleton and find a way to become an inker on my own.*

"Now you know you shouldn't be telling me such things," said Mr. Epiderm sharply, shocked out of signing. "You shouldn't even be thinking such things." He recomposed himself. *And anyway, such a plan would never work. The other inkers would not welcome you as a member if your own mother, who has been an inker for so many years, does not approve of your choice, and you know she would not, Firefly.*

Of course Firefly knew this very well. She had been thinking of ways to win her mother's support for years. It had never come close to happening. *I could leave this gorge, go to some place where they never heard of inking guilds and I could tattoo all the giants I want.*

Mr. Epiderm chuckled. *You are so sure of yourself,* he signed. *How do you even know giants exist elsewhere? And how do you know you can survive out of the gorge?*

It's where we're all supposed to go, signed Firefly.
What do you mean?
If the dam ever breaks, signed Firefly, *we're sup-*

posed to go out to sea to save ourselves. That's the plan, isn't it Mr. Epiderm?

Yes, of course, but it's just an emergency plan, signed Mr. Epiderm. *You can't base your life on a disaster. Now you heard your mother. She doesn't want you to ink and that's the end of the story. If you must leave Craddleton when you are older, you can always go downriver to Waffleton. That would be almost as good, wouldn't it?*

Firefly could not believe Mr. Epiderm was proposing such a ridiculous option. The people of Waffleton took the skins of deer and elk and made them into giant clothes. It was a necessary task, but it did not hold a candle to the romance of inking. Why, Mr. Epiderm might just as well have said she should go upriver and live among the salmon eaters in Dribbleton!

It's all so unfair, she signed to Mr. Epiderm. *My mother inks and her mother inked. We have had inkers in our family for generations. Why is it all of a sudden so awful for* me *to ink?*

The trade is very dangerous, signed Mr. Epiderm. He tapped his canes with his foot. *Surely I don't need to explain that to you. Your mother is very lucky she has not been injured. Fully three quarters of all inkers get some sort of serious injury while applying their ink. It's even dangerous for the giants. Once a giant came down here and tripped and fell so her head ended up in the river, unconscious. The water lapped at her nose and she was going to drown. I put my ink hoses in her nose and she was able to breath. Otherwise—* Mr. Epiderm raised his eyebrows and shrugged his shoulders.

"Wow," said Firefly, forgetting about signing. "You did that?"

Mr. Epiderm nodded. "Sideways thinking," he said, tapping his forehead. "I saw a problem and devised a way to use what I had in a new way to solve the problem. I released my assumptions about what the hoses were for."

"I want to do that!" said Firefly.

"Tell me," said Mr. Epiderm, "how is it that a girl such as yourself is so enamored of this particular profession? Most young people change their ambitions weekly. But not you."

Mr. Epiderm was right. Firefly's friend Mushroom was a perfect example. He would say he wanted to be a tailor to the giants one week, a scrubber of their teeth the next, and a groomer of their hair the week after that. He would clean out their ears, shave their chins, and brew their tea. He spoke of learning to cultivate their gardens, collect their dung, and bury their dead, even though these activities would entail going up on the plateau. Mushroom saw no limit to what he might do for the giants. Firefly told him he needed to settle down and decide on one thing. He said "Why, Firefly? What's so wonderful about wanting to do one thing?"

"If you are always doing all these different things," said Firefly, "you will never get good at any of them."

"How do you know?" said Mushroom. "I could be good at a million different things." He put out his arms and spread his hands. "I could be the greatest genius ever," he said.

Firefly rolled her eyes. "Oh yeah," she said. "My best friend is a genius."

"I could be. I might turn into a giant when I'm fifteen. I could be the smartest giant ever, with the biggest brain and the best ideas ever."

"Don't say that," said Firefly. "You won't be a giant."

Mushroom shrugged his shoulders. "I could be," he said.

"No," said Firefly. "Not you, Mushroom. Other boys, other kids, but not you. Or me."

"You know it could happen," said Mushroom. "It could happen to any of us."

"That would be awful."

"No it wouldn't. It would just be what happens. No one can control it, Firefly, so we have to accept what happens."

"If you became a giant, we wouldn't be best friends anymore."

Mushroom nodded. "That's what I mean," he

said. "That's just the way things would be."

Firefly hoped it never happened to Mushroom, but she mostly hoped it would never happen to her. The giants did almost nothing for themselves. That's why they took care of Firefly and the rest of the river people, who all attended to the needs of the giants. All except the people of Dribbleton, closer to the dam, who refused to be enslaved to the giants, which is the way they would say it, not the way Firefly thought of it. The people of Dribbleton were the poor people of the gorge, living in grubby little sod houses and scavenging for food as best they could, mostly from the river where they caught salmon, the very thought of which made Firefly wrinkle her nose in disgust. Eating those dying fish was about the most repulsive thing she could imagine.

The Dribbletonians never benefited from the generosity of the giants, who provided building materials for nice sturdy houses and also trapped and killed game like deer and elk with giant nets made of meshed vines mounted on big wooden hoops. The river people roasted the game on spits for magnificent meals down in the gorge all the time but the people of Dribbleton never did because they refused to accept any gifts from the giants. Such an attitude puzzled and distressed Firefly. Why would anyone refuse the generosity of the giants?

"Firefly?" said Mr. Epiderm. "Are you still with us?"

Firefly shook her head and came back to the present. "Mr. Epiderm," she said, "what was the best tattoo you ever did?"

Mr. Epiderm turned a little red. "Oh," he said, "that is such a long time past. No one cares what I inked so many years ago."

"I bet it was a picture of the sky, wasn't it Mr. Epiderm? You are always trying to get me to do my astronomy lessons because you love the stars so much. It was the sky, wasn't it Mr. Epiderm?"

"It is dangerous to draw conclusions about the past from present circumstances," said Mr. Epiderm. "Have I taught you nothing all these years?"

"OK," said Firefly. "Not the sky. Then it must have been a picture of one of the giant's sweethearts. Yes, you probably made it all fancy with grand colors and swooping hair. Isn't that it Mr. Epiderm? Wasn't that your best tattoo?"

Mr. Epiderm was about to say something, probably to try to steer the morning back to Firefly's lessons, when Mushroom burst through the front door, panting.

"Mushroom!" said Firefly. "What are you doing here?"

"It's your mother," said Mushroom. "One of the giants took her up the cliff."

THUNDER

Thunder awoke with a terrible itch on his chest, just to the left of his heart. Big gulps of air made it worse, so he forced himself to draw in shallow breaths. The other giants had told him the only relief for such pain was a tattoo.

He blinked away a dream about Fern, rose from his bed, shook away the crows that had settled in his hair during the night, stepped out of his cave, and began walking to the cliff. Patches of snow still clung to the sides of the trails. They would melt in a few days. The crows cawed around Thunder, then flapped off to look for food. Thunder raised his hand and waved, as though helping them on their way.

Thunder paused long enough to scoop up some water from his pond, slurping it with gusto, relishing the algae, turtle eggs, and slippery aquatic fronds as they went down his throat. He didn't much care for the bitter taste of frogs, but didn't go to the trouble of trying to spit them out of the pond water. Instead he crunched on their bones and swallowed quickly. Some of the pond water spilled out of his mouth and dripped down his shirt and the algae stained his teeth and lips. It was not, perhaps, the best of breakfasts, but it would sustain him well enough for the moment. Thunder dried his hands on his pants and continued walking.

He passed other caves, their doors closed. He knew giants lived in those caves, but he did not know most of them. That's what happened when you kept to yourself for so long. The last time he talked to another giant was when he and Moon had a shift together at the dam, helping to keep it in tip top condition. How long ago was that? A few weeks?

Moon had told him his tendency to isolate himself from others would pass. All new giants went through such a phase and it could last a long time. In Thunder's case it had been at least fourteen years since he began growing. So maybe it was about time for his first tattoo as a giant. It would join the firefly tattoo on his ankle which his sister Leaf had done when they were still pocket people.

Many of his neighbors never got the itch for tattoos anymore. Giants who had been tattooed over their entire bodies were now mostly very old or very eccentric. In any case, they were also very rare. In the past many giants had used the tattoos as a way of preserving their life stories—for as long as they remained alive at least, which, for giants, was quite a long time. Now many giants saw no use in preserving stories on their skins.

Thunder arrived at the cliff's edge and looked down to the gorge below. The pocket people had spread out over much of the land between the cliffs. Their settlements clung like beads on the string of the big river flowing placidly towards the sea, which was not visible from this distance. He saw Dribbleton next to the dam, his old home when he was still one of the pocket people. Downriver from there and immediately below him was Craddleton and then the rest of the villages: Wobbleton, Waffleton, Fabbleton, and much farther, almost out of view, Stubbleton, Buggleton, Paddleton, and others.

The river had once periodically roared through this gorge, washing away everything in its path. That ended when the giants built the dam, long before any people alive now, giant or pocket, had been born. Nowadays a big part of giant life was maintaining the dam. Without the dam no villages for the pocket people could exist: the big river would wash them all out to sea. The pocket people were so grateful to the giants for taming the erratic flow and making a home for them that they dedicated themselves to looking after the giants. For a long time that caretaking included the inking of tattoos on the giant's bodies.

Thunder followed the descending path through thickets of ferns and over rock outcroppings down to the gorge floor, where a clearing was available to the giants when they needed attention. Thunder dropped to his knees, which he knew would shake every house in the region, especially in Craddleton less than a mile away. He slowly turned himself over and let his back flop down on the ground. He tried as gently as he could—which wasn't very—to stretch out his legs and minimize the quakes. He let his hands drop to his sides. An inker would come soon.

A chill hung in the air. The sun had not yet warmed the gorge floor. Frost still coated the ground, but the heat of his body quickly melted the layer under his back and legs. He felt the vibrations of the waterfalls cascading down the cliffs on both sides of the gorge. The falls and streams flowing down the cliffs reminded him of ribs, and the big river in the center of the gorge made him think of a spine. Then what of the sea off in the unseen distance? Was it the head on the spine?

Thunder's imagination did not extend that far. Maybe the dam the giants had built years ago was the head? Who knew. He did not want to even think about the much bigger ice dam further upstream. He had never been there but he had heard stories. It was taller than ten giants, some said, an enormous glacier that defied anyone's imagination and kept most of the river far back. If the glacier ever melted and added its water to the river, nothing could stop it. It would smash through the giant's dam like a child's mud pie and the pocket people would all perish. So much water would flow that even some of the giants, though they lived high up on the plateau over the gorge, might be in danger from flooding.

Thunder had refrained from scratching the itch over his heart, but now, lying here quietly waiting for an inker, he could not help himself. He scraped his nails against his chest. At first he tried to keep from going too deep, but the temptation was irresistible and before long he was making deep gouges. It was the wrong thing to do but it felt so good to try to bring himself some relief. Not that it helped much. The itch was still there. He stopped himself.

He remembered this spot from when he was a boy and was still one of the pocket people. He used to come here with his sweetheart, Fern. In the summer they would bring a picnic lunch and sit and listen to the waterfalls on the cliff walls, that liquid sound, like voices singing. Later they would take a boat onto the big river and float along with the current. It was a wonderful time and Thunder still missed his days with Fern. In the evening they would capture the luminescent insects that flitted among the trees, hold them between their palms, and be mesmerized by the glow seeping out from between their fingers.

Those memories, though pleasant enough, also brought pain to Thunder. When he began growing just before his fifteenth birthday, Fern became almost like a stranger to him. His life with the pocket people was over. As he gained stature, they all turned away from him. His friends told him they could not be his friends any longer. Fern ignored him completely. His family said it was time for him to go, as his sister had gone months before, and he should get about it quickly for everyone's sake. Thunder had known others who had become giants. It was always a possibility.

He had not seen his family since he moved up from the gorge and into his life as a giant. His parents still lived in Dribbleton, in the shadow of the dam. He could see them, sometimes, tiny people in decrepit houses. Why didn't they see how caring for the giants was the way to prosperity and happiness? And why couldn't they see that even as a giant he was still worth loving? They are stubborn, thought Thunder. Stubborn and ridiculous.

He felt a jab at his elbow and looked down. An inker stood next to him with a long branch. She dropped the branch and raised her other hand, which held an inking tool, to show she was ready to go. She wore heavy overalls and she had her ink supply strapped to her back. Thunder made a fist and extended his thumb. The inker signed a question: *Where?*

Thunder moved his fingers jerkily and angled his hands so the inker could see what he was signing: *Over my heart.* He unbuttoned his shirt, and put his hand, palm down, on the ground next to the pocket person. Some inkers liked help getting up. Others preferred their own muscle power with the assistance of ladders, many of which leaned against the cliff nearby for easy access. Thunder was reasonably sure this one would accept his assistance, which she did. She stepped up on his hand and laid down, with her arms and legs outstretched for stability. Thunder raised her slowly and carefully and put his palm against his chest. The inker jumped off his hand and stood on his sternum. Thunder put his finger on the site of his itch. The inker put her hands on her hips and surveyed the area.

You've been scratching, she signed.
Couldn't help it.

The inker looked at him. Her face registered

caring and pity. *I understand,* she signed.

As her hands formed the words of sympathy, a rush of recognition flooded Thunder's being. Could it be? He had not seen Fern in years, and yet he could not mistake her face or her figure. He looked again, studying her features carefully. Yes. The inker was Fern, his old sweetheart from when he was one of the pocket people. He had not known she had become an inker. He could scarcely contain his excitement, but knew he had to keep very still for her own protection. Did she know? How could she?

When pocket people became giants they looked completely different, which meant Fern could not possibly recognize him. Thunder's whole body had thickened to support the weight of his new mass. His legs distorted into giant pillars, his arms thickened into tree trunks, his hands became stumps with stubby roots. His nose grew bulbous and his eye sockets more hooded. His neck was much thicker in proportion to his head. He lost most of his voice, able now only to make incoherent sounds. And he had become deaf. His ears had elongated so his lobes hung down almost to his shoulders. The pocket people considered giants to be rather ugly. But Fern was no different from before. She looked just as beautiful.

What image? signed Fern.

Thunder hesitated.

Fern signed some suggestions. *Tree? Dragon? River? Crow? What have you been dreaming?*

Do you remember how we used to look at the moon? signed Thunder.

Fern frowned. *You want the moon? What phase?*

You always liked three quarter full. Like it is now. Never completely full. You said you always wanted something to look forward to. Remember?

Fern looked as though she wanted to run away, but she was stuck on Thunder's chest, and a pocket person couldn't simply jump off a giant's chest and walk away. She signed a question. *Thunder?*

Yes. It's me.

She stood for a long time, feet unmoving, breaths coming in shallow spurts. *I didn't know you still lived above Craddleton. I thought you might have moved on.*

I should have. But I couldn't. Would you like to come up the cliff? I'd love to talk to you for a while.

Fern looked around. Her eyes followed the wall of the cliff to the top edge, fringed with the dusty green of conifers. *Up?*

Yes.

We don't go up.

You could.

Why would I?

Thunder had no answer. He just wanted her to see where he lived. *I'll bring you right back,* he signed. *Promise.*

Fern pointed down to Thunder's chest. *What about your tattoo?*

It can wait.

Why would you talk to me, signed Fern, *after I stopped talking to you?*

That was a long time ago. We were young. You didn't know any better.

Fern hesitated a few seconds. *OK,* she signed.

Thunder helped Fern to the ground, then worked laboriously to button up his shirt. Fern took off her ink canisters and dropped them to the ground. Thunder put them against the cliff wall next to the ladders for safe keeping, hitting a ladder as he did so and splintering it into two pieces.

Sorry, he signed.

It's nothing, signed Fern. Thunder put down his hand. Fern climbed up on it and Thunder lifted her up to his shirt pocket, which he pulled open with his other hand. Fern jumped from his palm into the pocket. She scrambled to right herself and poked her head above the top edge of the pocket, which she grabbed with both hands to keep herself steady. She wedged her feet firmly on the bottom seam. She was a perfect fit.

Thunder put his hand up where Fern could see. *Comfortable?* he signed.

Yes.

Thunder began climbing back up the path, planting each foot with a cliff-shaking tremor. When they reached the top, Thunder stood to catch his breath. Fern poked at him through the shirt. Thunder looked down.

By the way, signed Fern. *I probably should have told you a long time ago.*

Yes?

You have a daughter.

firefly

"What do you mean a giant took my mother?" said Firefly. No one with any sense went up to the plateau where the giants lived. The giants did not like it.

"It's true," said Mushroom. "I saw it myself."

"Young man," said Mr. Epiderm. "If you are not telling us the truth—"

Mushroom shook his head vigorously. "Oh no, Mr. Epiderm," he said. "I'm not lying. I saw it. I saw it with my own eyes."

Firefly stood up. "If this is some kind of dumb joke—"

"Why doesn't anyone believe me?" said Mushroom. "Come with me and you'll see."

Firefly turned to Mr. Epiderm. He waved his hand at her. "Go, go," he said. "You have to see if it's true."

Firefly and Mushroom flew out the door and

kept running. They ran toward the big river, scattering flocks of crows as they went, then over the bridge, their feet thumping on the wooden slats. They angled toward a stream on the other side of the bridge and followed it to the foot of the cliff where Firefly's mother would usually tattoo the giants. They came to a stop. Firefly looked around. She saw the sand had been recently disturbed by a giant, and she saw her mother's ink canisters and needle propped against the cliff wall beside the ladders. She also saw a ladder broken in two. The pieces lay on the sand. Firefly ran to the ladder and bent down to examine it. Mushroom stood beside her.

"Why is this ladder broken?" she said.

"The giant did it by accident," said Mushroom.

"He shouldn't be breaking ladders. He's way too clumsy, even for a giant. Mushroom, I'm worried. Where's my mother?"

"The giant took her up the cliff," said Mushroom. "That's what I've been trying to tell you. She went up in his pocket."

"What were you doing here?" she said.

"I like seeing the giants come down," said Mushroom. "I sit over there"—he pointed to a copse of cottonwoods near the stream's edge—"and watch them. They are so amazing."

"And then he just grabbed my mother?"

"Not exactly," said Mushroom. "She climbed up on his hand and he put her in his pocket."

"That's impossible!" said Firefly. "My mother wouldn't get into a giant's pocket. She would never go up the cliff with a giant."

"I'm just telling you what I saw," said Mushroom.

Firefly looked up the face of the cliff. It was covered in ferns, moss, and a few small trees. Taller ones were too heavy to cling to the face with its steep angle. The path the giants took was not made for people of her size. The crevices and depressions were too wide for river people. Most gorge dwellers considered it foolish to try to climb any of the cliffs.

"We have to go up," said Firefly.

"Up?" said Mushroom.

"Yes," said Firefly. "Yes yes. We have to see what happened to my mother."

"I'm sure she's ok," said Mushroom.

"She's not ok," said Firefly. "She can't be ok on the plateau. My mother is in trouble. I have to go find her."

"It's too dangerous," said Mushroom. "Just wait. Your mother will come back. Probably in the giant's pocket."

Firefly doubted that. It didn't make any sense for her mother to go with the giant voluntarily. "What would make her *want* to go up there with a giant?" she asked Mushroom.

Mushroom shrugged. "I don't know."

Firefly turned from him and looked up. She had to bend her head way back to see the top lip of the cliff. Only a few minutes ago Fern was telling Mr. Epiderm how she wanted to go up on the plateau and live among the giants. Now that thought felt like the most foolish thing she could ever imagine saying or doing. She couldn't live there. She had to get her mother back. Firefly scanned the cliff. She searched for a path, looking for crevices where she could put her hands and feet. The ones she saw were far apart, and the overhanging rocks looked impossible to get around. She followed some paths for a while. They ended where she could not see a way forward.

"Even if you get to the top," said Mushroom, "what will you do? You don't know where she is."

"I'll find her," said Firefly. "Are you coming with me or not?"

"We can't go up here."

"I know it's impossible," said Firefly. "That's not going to stop me."

Mushroom studied Firefly's face carefully. "Come here with me," he said. He began walking quickly along the sand away from the clearing. Firefly hurried to catch up with him.

"I'm going," she said. "Don't try to stop me."

"Stop you?" said Mushroom. "How could I ever stop you?"

They came to a wooded area carpeted with thick underbrush. Mushroom plunged right into the bramble and Firefly, hesitating only for a second, followed. They elbowed their way through shrubs and more ferns than Firefly knew even existed. "Where are you taking me?" she said.

"Just keep going," said Mushroom. "You'll see in a minute."

The woods gave way to another sandy clearing against the cliff. A few lengths of vines hung on the cliff face. "What's this?" said Firefly.

"I found these a long time ago. They are strong vines." Mushroom took one in his hand and tugged on it. It held fast. "I think you can get to the plateau on these," he said.

Firefly tested a couple of the vines herself. They felt completely secure. They also had something sticky on them. Firefly pulled her hand away. "What's this?" she said, displaying her palm to Mushroom.

"Sap," said Mushroom. "The vines sweat it out and bugs like the smell so they land on it and stick to it and then they get absorbed into the vines. It's how the vines eat."

Firefly took hold of the vine again and looked

up. She saw crows circling way up where her vision registered only blurs. "Do these vines go all the way to the top?" she asked.

"Yeah," said Mushroom. "I think they grow from up on the plateau and hang down."

"You *think*?"

"I don't know for sure."

"You mean you haven't been up these vines?"

"No. I'm too scared."

Firefly smiled. "My best friend is too scared?"

"It's a long way up," said Mushroom.

Firefly, still holding the vine, put her foot on the cliff face and raised herself off the ground. It was an awkward stance. She was parallel to the ground, but the sticky sap helped her hang on. She was sure she could climb to the top using these vines as aids. She snaked up a few more feet. If she tried to pull her hands away quickly, the sap held her tight. But if she relaxed her muscles for a few seconds she could release her arms and legs and grab the vine higher and pull herself up. Before long she was twenty feet above Mushroom. She wrapped the vine around her arms and legs and hung suspended over the ground. "Are you coming?" she said.

Mushroom looked up at her. "I don't know," he said.

"You don't have to," said Firefly. "I can find my

mother on my own. Go tell Mr. Epiderm what I'm doing."

"Do you think he'll believe me?"

"Just go, Mushroom."

He stood gawking for another second or two, then bolted and ran toward Craddleton. Firefly watched him go. Was she going to do this alone? She looked up along the length of her vine and could not see the top edge of the cliff. It had to be there, though, somewhere beyond the blur of clinging ferns and diminishing vines. If it took her a minute to go twenty feet, and if she rested after each minute for thirty seconds or so, it would take her a little bit over half an hour to get to the top. She hoped that would be fast enough to get her mother back.

Firefly tried not to think about those problems. She needed to focus on one thing at a time, and right now it was climbing. She unstuck her legs from the vine, planted them firmly on the cliff wall, and raised herself up with her arms. Fortunately for her, she was a small person, only three feet tall, with not much in the way of extra weight. The vine retained its stickiness as she ascended.

As Firefly climbed, and the gorge floor receded, she grew a little dizzy from the new perspective. She told herself she would not look down. Instead, she looked only at the wall in front of her. It was mostly rock, good solid areas for her to plant her feet. The vine grew thicker as she climbed.

The air was completely still up here. Quiet. Crows circled near her. A lot of crows. Why were crows collecting into big flocks? They never used to do that. Now they were always gathering and flying to the dam and beyond.

Firefly paused and clung to her vine. Small grottos punctuated the cliff wall here. As she climbed past them she saw some with nests. It was spring, and birds were getting ready to lay their eggs. She calculated she had been climbing for about twenty minutes when the vine began thickening very dramatically, and soon she arrived at the root of the vine. It had sprung out of a crevice in the rock. Now what? thought Firefly. She clung to the vine and looked around.

Below her many river people had gathered in a half circle near the copse of trees where she began her climb. She thought she saw Mushroom among them, but could not be sure. Had he told everyone in Craddleton? It sure looked that way, and maybe everyone else in the gorge too, since Firefly saw more people crossing the bridge over the big river to join the crowd. Some were shouting. She could not make out what most were saying, but she thought she heard snatches of phrases. "—is she craz—" "—come down—" "—irefly be —"

Firefly, stuck to the vine, began feeling a burning sensation along her legs and arms. Also on her chest. All the places where the vine came in contact with her. The vines must eat the insects by dissolving them with some caustic secretion, like burning acid, which Firefly knew people and animals had in their stomachs, and which this vine must have had on its surface. It was a mild acid, but strong enough to do in insects and strong enough to cause discomfort to a fourteen-year-old girl after she had been exposed to it for some time.

Firefly looked wildly around for another vine. She saw a thinner one nearby and reached for it. It was too far away. She looked at her hand. It was so red it looked like it had been burned. And it was starting to itch. Firefly wanted to release the vine right then and there. But she could not. If she did, she would fall and be smashed on the gorge floor far below.

THUNDER

Thunder stood on the top edge of the cliff, with Fern still in his pocket looking up at him. A daughter? He had a daughter? He scarcely knew what to think about that. He began walking to his cave. Fern poked at his chest. He looked down at her. *Did you understand what I just signed?*

He nodded and kept walking.

Don't you want to know her name?

Was it important to know her name? She could never be a real daughter to him anyway, and he could never be a real father to her. They were from different worlds now. Thunder didn't answer Fern. He didn't want to. She must have gotten pregnant just before he started becoming a giant. No wonder she wanted nothing to do with him. The father of her child was becoming giant, turning into a completely alien—not to mention repulsive—creature. What mother would want her child to know a father who would always be separate from her?

Still, Fern could have told him at the time. He wouldn't have interfered. He knew, even at such a young age, that his life was to be elsewhere. He sighed. What was he thinking bringing Fern up here? Giants did not normally want pocket people in their realm, getting underfoot. Too much chance of stepping on them, and even the most diligent of efforts to be careful could not prevent accidents from happening. What could he hope to understand about his life, or hers, by bringing her here?

Thunder felt Fern poking at him. She had more to tell him, but Thunder was not ready to listen. He stopped. Maybe it was best to go back down the cliff, leave Fern there, and forget about the pocket people, at least for now. He felt her hanging onto the lip of his shirt. He found comfort in having her with him, remembering their days together. The itch on his chest that had sent him down the cliff in the first place was mostly gone now. How could that be, without the tattoo to soothe it away?

He looked down at Fern. She stared up at him. *You have the most enormous nose in the world*, she signed. *I can see right up into it from here. If it wasn't about the most disgusting thing I could imagine, I'm pretty sure I could take up residence in one of your nostrils.*

Thunder laughed. Fern covered her ears until Thunder stopped laughing. *Quite a chortle you have there,* she signed.

Thunder laughed again. *OK,* he signed. *Tell me her name.*

Fern cupped one hand over her other.

Thunder blinked. *You named her Firefly?* he signed.

Fern nodded.

Thunder felt tears well up in his eyes. Firefly. His daughter was named Firefly. The thought of her name made him feel proud, sad, happy, and lost all at the same time.

What is she like? he signed. *Is she smart?*

She's too smart for her own good sometimes. She also does things on a whim. I never know what she's going to be getting up to next.

Oh that's wonderful. Is she good at sports?

She doesn't much go for sports, but she's strong. She's also stubborn, like you. She wants to be an inker and nothing I say can change her mind.

What's wrong with being an inker?

You all are so clumsy. You kill half of us. Also, you don't even want tattoos anymore. I want her to make giant clothes. It's safe and there will always be a demand.

Thunder had to correct the exaggeration. *We don't kill half of you,* he signed.

OK, not half. Still. Close to it.

Not that close.

OK, ok. You only kill a few.

Also, signed Thunder, *most of the injuries are due to your own carelessness.*

I don't know that we want to get into this debate now, signed Fern. *And anyway, what does it matter? Inking is dangerous, that's all. She's my only daughter.*

Yes, thought Thunder. And mine.

Are we close to your cave yet? signed Fern. *This is not the most comfortable of traveling arrangements.*

Soon, signed Thunder. He hurried his pace, kicking down trees as he went by, shaking the ground, setting off earthquakes.

His cave was set in a hill behind a stand of pines. As they approached his pond, he felt pride and wanted Fern to notice it. He had excavated the pond himself when he first became a giant and was newly arrived on the plateau. The digging and shaping of the earth, the channelling of streams of water into the depression, it was all a way to keep himself busy and forget his previous life. It was a way to make himself believe he was a giant. Some of the other giants tried to help him then, but he had not wanted their help. He had been something of a hermit for many years now, needing the time to come to grips with his new situation. The deafness was the hardest part. Not being able to hear the world. How could anyone live this way?

There were some consolations for the deafness. He could expect a very long life. The plateau held more numerous and more beautiful wildlife than the gorge. Deer and elk were abundant, as were the berries that made his mouth water. When he first tasted pond algae he was sure it would make him sick, but it turned out that as a giant he was perfectly suited to it. It became one of the foods he most enjoyed, and he set up drying racks for it so he could have it as a snack whenever he wanted.

Those racks lined the path on the way to the cave. Thunder pulled open the enormous door, which he had fashioned out of logs from trees he had felled himself, and stepped inside. The door scraped against the ground and was not a perfect fit in the cave entrance—large gaps let in crows and bats—but it was good enough for him. He put his hand next to the top of his pocket. Fern climbed out of the pocket and fell onto Thunder's palm. He carried her to the table, where she jumped off his palm and sat cross-legged on the wooden tabletop. She looked up at the ceiling, which was at least thirty times her body length. Thunder followed her gaze. His ceiling must be another sky to her. Sunlight streamed through an opening at the top.

You have a lovely home, she signed. *Very roomy.*

Thanks, said Thunder. She stared at him. *Oh,* he signed, *that was a joke.*

Something like that.

I don't often have visitors, and never one of your wit or stature, so I'm not used to your jokes. Or any jokes. I don't have much in the cave—house—that's your size. Would you like some tea? I make it from dried algae.

Fern wrinkled her nose.

Thunder laughed quietly, out of deference to Fern's tiny ears. *You should try it.*

OK. she signed. *Then I need to be going.*

Thunder looked at her. *Going?*

Yes, going. Firefly will worry about me if I don't get back soon.

Thunder picked up a bowl filled with water and some of his dried algae from a table illuminated by the rays of light coming through his skylight. He had put it there the day before to let his tea steep in the sun.

He took a wooden spoon from the cupboard, stuck to the cave wall with mud and grass, and dipped the spoon into the bowl to fill it with his algae tea. He put the spoon down in front of Fern. It was enormous next to her. Green liquid splashed out of it and dripped down the side. Thunder was acutely conscious of trying to be very careful as he moved. He wanted so much to make a good impression on Fern and was not even sure why.

Thank you, signed Fern.

You're welcome.

Fern bent forward over the spoon, as though she was bending close to a stream's edge, and used her hands to lift up some of the deep green liquid to her mouth. She took a sip. Thunder watched anxiously to see if she liked it. She stared into space as she rolled the liquid around in her mouth, swallowed, and immediately bent down for some more.

You like it! signed Thunder.

Fern took more swallows. *It's very good. I never would have thought. The color is like the pine trees on the edge of the cliff. I always like seeing that glorious green towering over us.*

If you're a giant, it helps to like algae. It's very common around here.

We have some in the gorge. Maybe I'll start making my own tea.

The thought pleased Thunder. *You should do that,* he signed. *Maybe you might even try fish.*

Fern's eyes narrowed. *Fish? Never.*

Because the Dribbletonians like it?

Fern hesitated. *No. That's not why.*

I was from Dribbleton, remember?

Yes, of course I remember.

Eating fish is not a terrible thing.

I know that too, signed Fern. *I just don't like it.*

Thunder nodded, signing nothing. His hands hovered in the air, unmoving.

Fern tried to get the conversation going again.

Whatever happened to your sister? she signed. *Do you ever see her?*

No, signed Thunder. *Soon after Leaf became giant, she disappeared. She lived up here for a while, then she was gone. It still makes me sad, not knowing what happened to her.*

Oh, said Fern, instantly regretting asking a question so distressing to Thunder. *Maybe Leaf's in a better place,* she signed.

I doubt it, signed Thunder, *but I suppose it is remotely possible she has at least some happiness, wherever she is.*

Fern nodded. She needed to find some other topic for discussion, and fast. *You don't have a lot of snow left up here,* she signed. *I always thought you giants had snow a lot longer than we did.*

Thunder filled a cup of his own with some of the algae tea and sat down at the table. *The melts have been coming earlier every year,* he signed. He was careful to keep his elbows away from Fern, who still sat near the center of the table.

Why is that happening? signed Fern.

Thunder shrugged. *I don't know. We've had lots more little tremors, too. Way more than we are responsible for.*

We've noticed too, signed Fern. *Anyone know what that's about?*

Thunder shrugged. *Nope.* He took a sip of his

tea. *I think a lot of pocket people would like this tea.*

Pocket people? signed Fern.

That's what we call you. Didn't you know?

I had no idea.

Oh yes.

What else do you say about us?

Oh, not much. We say you are cute and we like how hard working you are. We like seeing the gorge filled up with you and your little villages. It's charming. We like you, you know, even though a lot of you don't like us much.

Fern frowned. *That's not true. Some of you scare us. That's not the same thing at all.*

It feels the same. What have you told Firefly about us?

I have always told her giants are like any other people. There are good ones and bad ones, but if you try to understand them, you'll find they are mostly good, like anybody else.

No, signed Thunder. *I mean what have you told her about us. You and me.*

Fern's hands remained unmoving in the air, stuck on the word for "else."

Fern? signed Thunder.

I haven't told her anything.

Oh. So she doesn't know who her father is?

I told her her father died.

Oh.

It's complicated, signed Fern.

Doesn't seem complicated to me.

I was so young, signed Fern. *Too young to have a child. And you were going away. Once you became giant, she didn't have a father. Not in any way that mattered.*

Of course it would have been an impossible situation for Thunder to try to be a father to Firefly. Still, it hurt to know Fern could so easily delete him from her life. *I suppose I understand,* he said.

Fern bit her lip. *Do you have a girlfriend up here?*

Thunder shook his head. *All that girl boy stuff disappears for giants.*

I didn't know, signed Fern. *I mean, lots of us thought so, but no one knew for sure.*

Yup. Everything changes. Our whole physical makeup. Life is different for giants. Do you remember that song you used to hum? How did it go?

Fern frowned. *You mean the tune?*

No, the words. What were they?

In morning light, my heart's delight is slinking in and inking skin. To draw the fire of your heart's desire; to break your bones and hear your moans.

Yes, that's it, signed Thunder. *Did you ever wonder about those last lines? Why would an inker want to break bones? Why would an inker want to hear moans?*

It's a lullaby, signed Fern. *It's not supposed to make sense. Anyway, a lot of lullabies have things like that in them. There are ones where babies fall from trees and where they get diseases and curl up and die. That's just what lullabies do.*

Yes, I know, but the song isn't about the baby getting hurt, it's about hurting the giant. Did you ever wonder about that?

It's you guys, the giants, that break our bones, signed Fern. *We couldn't break a giant bone if we tried, and none of us want to try. Plus, you get to live forever.*

No, signed Thunder. *Not forever.*

A long time, then. I think I hated that most of all when you became a giant. I was going to shrivel up and croak, but you were going to keep on living year after year after year. It still makes me mad, thinking you will outlive Firefly.

So the song is a wish? It's something you can't do, so you imagine doing it?

Fern shook her head. *Who knows? Why are you so interested in that song?*

The table started shaking. The spoon bounced and skittered across the table top and so did Fern. She put out her arms to try to steady herself. The tea spilled out of the spoon and spread out on the table.

Fern held up her hands. *What in blue thunderation is that?*

Just some of my neighbors passing by.

The tremors did not stop. Thunder realized something was not right. A certain amount of shaking in the earth was inevitable when giants walked by, but these quakes were excessive. It was as though his neighbors were running. Giants, as a rule, did not run. They were not made for it. Fern was still skittering across the table. Thunder put down his hand to keep her from falling over the edge. She wrapped her arms around his thumb and hung on. He lifted her up to his shirt pocket, she jumped inside and Thunder stepped through his doorway to the outside. Several giants were hurrying past his house.

What's going on? signed Fern.

I don't know, signed Thunder.

One of the giants came down the path to Thunder's cave. She stopped, barely glancing at Fern in Thunder's shirt pocket, but long enough to register surprise. *It's the dam,* she signed. *It's starting to collapse. Come help us. The pocket people are all in peril.*

firefly

The burns on Firefly's hands were getting more itchy by the second. She felt panic begin to paralyze her. That was not good. If she let fear take over she would be in even worse trouble. She tried to calm her breathing and think of her dilemma as a story problem. She was good at story problems.

She remembered from one of Mr. Epiderm's lessons that when you contract an irritation or inflammation in nature, the cure for it was usually nearby. She never understood exactly what he meant by that. Maybe now was a good time to figure it out.

The basics first: she had contacted an acidic sap and it was irritating her. Which meant, if Mr. Epiderm was right, and he was very rarely not right, a cure for her itch was close by. She hung from the vine and looked around. Maybe she should rub a rock on the red patches. She put out one hand

and placed it palm down on the rock next to the vine. It was slightly damp, a little cooler than the air. It didn't offer her anything in the way of relief. Crows circled around her, cawing and kicking up a fuss. What's wrong with the crows today? she wondered. They were everywhere and they were more restless than she had ever known them to be.

Forget about the crows, she thought. Focus on your problem.

What about the moss? Maybe. Some patches of moss clung on the rock a few feet below her. She descended on the vine and put her hand against a bright green clump of the cushiony softness. It was warmer than the rock, but the irritation didn't feel any better. All she wanted to do was scratch it. She kept herself from succumbing to the urge. She was sure that would only make it worse.

Mr. Epiderm was always trying to get her to understand sideways thinking. It's when you step out of the problem and look at it from a different view and you do it when you're sure your problem has no solution. It was all about identifying your hidden assumptions and turning them upside down and sideways.

Firefly looked up. The top of the cliff was out of her view. She looked down. People were still gathered on the gorge floor, looking up at her. What was sideways thinking in this situation? She imagined all the people below her were crows, which meant they were now above her. At the same time she imagined the top edge of the cliff as the shore of the big river. Which meant the cliff was now below her. The sky was beneath her, the gorge soaring above her. She had been climbing up, and now, by sideways thinking, she was climbing down.

Even though it made no sense at all, it gave her an idea. She went back the way she came, along the vine to the thinner part, down to where she had seen the grotto. She put one foot on the lip of the rock, waited a couple of seconds, released the sticky vine, and stepped into the grotto. She had enough room to stretch out. The cave did not appear to go very far in, but it was enough to hold her for now and keep her relatively safe from any immediate disaster. She was still worried about her mother. If she could get this burn taken care of, maybe she could crawl out of the grotto and find another vine to climb.

It was dark in the cave. She turned around and put her face over the edge and looked down at the gorge floor. She waved. Some of her neighbors, still gathered below, waved back. She shouted as loud as she could. "I'm ok. Don't come up for me."

She saw some crows eating bugs from the vines. They were such opportunists. Instead of hunting for their own food, they let the vine capture their lunch, then they swooped in and ate it. Crows were the experts at sideways thinking, always figuring out ways to get other creatures and plants to work for them. How did they get the bugs from the vines without getting burned?

Firefly felt around in the cave. Moisture coated some of the rock. Water dripped from the ceiling. A few tiny stalactites hung there. Towards the back, where the rocks contracted to a small gap, she saw a nest. She crawled over to it. Empty. No, not quite. Feathers and pieces of shell littered the bottom. The babies must have hatched already. The nest was made of twigs and leaves, with some strands of thread mixed in—probably from the clothes makers in Waffleton—and cemented together with some kind of glue. Now where would the birds have gotten this glue? Did they find it down in the gorge, or up on the giant's plateau?

Sideways thinking, thought Firefly. *If ever I needed sideways thinking it's now.*

Everyone had hidden assumptions. It was the way human brains worked. She knew she had a hidden assumption about the glue. What was it? That the glue came from somewhere else. Well, maybe it didn't. Maybe it came from right here. She ran her hand over the ceiling of the grotto. She encountered stalactites and more dampness. Some moss. A few tiny ferns, probably starved for light stuck inside this cave. A few spiders skittered away from her. Nothing sticky up here. Nothing that could be a glue of any kind.

Firefly picked up the nest and held it close to her nose. Definitely not mud. It had the unmistakable heaviness and startling richness of animal waste. So the crows used dung to cement their nests. But whose dung? She did not recognize the odor. Certainly not river person or giant. It had to come from somewhere, either the gorge or the plateau.

Hidden assumptions. Hidden assumptions. What do I believe that isn't so? Firefly answered her own question. *That I need to know where the dung came from. It doesn't* matter *where it came from.*

Firefly turned the nest over. Feathers fluttered to the grotto floor. She put her hand on the bottom of the nest. Immediately her burning sensation began to soothe. "Ahhh," she whispered to herself. "That's the answer. They keep from getting burned on the vines by their own droppings." Firefly broke the nest into pieces, pulled out some of the bigger twigs and applied the pieces to each of the places where her skin burned. The relief was almost instantaneous. Firefly put chunks of the nest into her pockets.

She stuck her head out of the grotto again and looked first up, then down. All she had to do was descend a short distance and she would be close to a thinner vine. She could climb that one to the top.

She wrapped herself around the vine again, and slipped down about fifteen feet, reached over as far as she could, snagged the thinner vine, and swung herself over onto it.

She glanced down at the gorge floor. The people from Craddleton shouted at her. "Stay up." "Firefly, don't come down."

Now that was odd. Why did they want her to stay on the cliff when only a few minutes ago they wanted her to come back down? The crowd had dissipated some, but many more people were running out of Craddleton and toward the cliff. They ran toward the copse of trees where Mushroom had shown her the vines. They wanted to climb the vines? Like her?

Firefly climbed twenty or thirty feet. She stopped to rest. Upriver, toward the dam, she saw people running from Dribbleton. Some ran downstream toward Craddleton, and others ran upstream toward the dam. People in the gorge did not, as a rule, go running all over the place like they were droplets careening off a waterfall.

Firefly squinted toward the river. I looked wider than normal. How strange. Why would the river suddenly get wider? She looked downstream towards where the river eventually met the sea. Yes, it definitely looked bigger than she remembered. She followed the line of the river with her eye, back upstream toward the dam. At first she couldn't tell what she was seeing. It looked like thick black smoke rising from the dam. She strained her eyes and saw hundreds, maybe thousands, of crows circling above the dam. They landed in groups behind the dam, out of her view, stayed for a few seconds, then rose and descended again.

And then Firefly saw a sight she had hoped she would never see: A waterfall at the dam. Sometimes, especially in the spring, a tiny trickle came over the top of the dam, barely enough to make the big river rise a tiny bit. But now the water spilling over the top of the dam dislodged some of the enormous rocks the giants had placed to keep the river back. Several of the rocks had tumbled to the bottom of the dam, so close to Dribbleton she thought some of their houses might have been crushed. Firefly blinked several times, trying to make her mind accept what she was seeing.

The dam was failing, and all the people of the gorge were in trouble.

Where were the giants? They should all be on the scene, taking care of the dam. Where *were* they?

Firefly's heart beat wildly. She moved up the vine like a startled spider. She didn't take any more rests. Within a few minutes the vine she was climbing began thickening. She was getting to the root end. She saw another vine a short distance to her left. She reached for it with her leg and arm. The new vine stuck to her. She released the old vine and wrapped herself around the new vine and kept going up. Finally the vertical face of the cliff receded a little, rounding out in a smooth arc. She got to the thickest part of the vine. It was rooted in the rocks. No other vines hung nearby. It didn't matter. She had come to the top of the cliff. She was no longer in the gorge. She was on the giant's plateau. She walked up the last few feet, over the rounded edge of rock to a forested area of tall evergreens.

Firefly wasted no time admiring their color or stature. She ran along the edge of the cliff, weaving around trees. Before long she came to a wide path that had been flattened to a hard surface without any vegetation, probably from years of giant feet trampling it down. In one direction the path went to the edge of the cliff overlooking the gorge. In the other direction? Firefly had no idea, but guessed it must be where the giants lived.

She stepped off the forest floor, littered with bramble and alive with a frenzy of ferns, and began walking on the path, away from the cliff's edge. She walked in footprints, giant footprints. Were they made by the giant who took her mother? Firefly began to trot along the path. As she ran, she felt tremors in the ground. They quickly grew more severe. To keep from stumbling and falling, she had to be careful as she placed her feet. Soon she began to hear branches snapping off in the distance. The sound of branches falling approached her rapidly. She was sure she heard trees being felled as well. A tremendous crash reverberated in the air. She looked up and saw giants in the distance. Several of them. No, more than a dozen. And they were all running toward the dam, which Firefly recognized as a good thing because they might save the dam and the gorge.

Only one problem. Firefly was directly underfoot, exactly in the path between the advancing giants and the crumbling dam. She calculated, on the spot, that she did not have enough time to run back to the cliff's edge where she would be the safest. Instead, it looked like she would have to wait right where she was, right where any of a couple of dozen giant feet could come down on her and crush her to death.

THUNDER

The giant turned from Thunder and Fern and rejoined the other giants hurrying toward the dam. Thunder looked down at his pocket.

I have to go help, he signed.

Of course, signed Fern.

I'll leave you in my cave.

No, signed Fern. *I need to go back to Craddleton to make sure Firefly is safe.*

You can't go down the cliff on your own.

Fern chewed her lip. *You'll have to take me.*

I can't, he signed. *The best thing for everyone is if I go help with the dam. Everyone is in trouble now, not only Firefly. If we save the dam, we save everyone, including Firefly.*

Fern looked in the direction of the cliff. *I don't know,* she signed.

Thunder had no more patience. *Look,* he signed, *giants are running around everywhere. Do you want to be killed by one?*

Fern shook her head.

Then wait here, he signed. *I have to go.*

Will I be safe?

You mean if I don't come back?

She hesitated. *Something like that, yes.*

I'll come back. Don't worry. But just in case, I'll leave the door open so you can go if you need to. Wait until the giants are gone. Thunder went into the cave and got a clean wooden bowl from the cupboard and put it on the floor. He put his hand up to his pocket. Fern climbed on and Thunder moved his hand down to the bowl. Fern slid off Thunder's hand into the bowl.

How does that feel? signed Thunder. *I want to put you up on a cupboard, but then you couldn't get down by yourself.* The bowl vibrated against the floor. Still a lot of giants running around.

No, leave me here so I can get out if I need to.

Be careful if you do.

Don't worry about me, signed Fern. *Go. Fix the dam.*

Thunder looked down at her. She was so small, so fragile. Was it possible he was once so small? *Bye,* he signed.

Go, Thunder. You need to go now.

He turned from her and went outside. Giants still hurried by, but fewer than before. Most of them must already be at the dam. He followed the path along the edge of the cliff. Crows flew toward the dam. Why were the crows following the giants? They usually had their own agenda, and it never included paying attention to what the giants were doing.

Thunder glanced over his shoulder. Giants walked behind him and giants walked ahead of him. He thought of himself as running, but realized it would be more accurate to call his gait a somewhat speeded up trot. Giants were not capable of running in the same way pocket people ran. Their huge mass made it difficult to coordinate the actions necessary for true running. Also, it took too much work to move so much weight. Thunder never saw so many giants moving so quickly.

Soon the dam came into view. Thunder was truly startled by what he saw.

Pocket people from Dribbleton streamed up from the gorge floor, trying to get to higher ground, he supposed, and doing it by climbing toward the dam and going up the side. Was the dam in such serious trouble the pocket people had to abandon their homes? And what were all the crows doing there? Huge flocks of them, like dark clouds, hovered over the dam. On the plateau, giants carried thirty foot rocks and plunked them down in the stream going over the top of the dam. Other giants scooped up great mounds of earth and wedged them between the rocks. Still other giants covered the dam with tree branches and swatches of ferns. They pushed them into the mud between the rocks, all in an attempt to shore up the crumbling dam.

Giants were clumsy creatures, but when a task like the collapsing of the dam needed attending to, they got into a rhythm that worked. Thunder waded into the fray. He walked a short distance from the dam to where the giants had started a boulder quarry in what had once been a hill. A lot of rock still remained in the hill.

Thunder joined a few other giants and began to scrape earth out of the quarry. When he had excavated a couple of dozen feet down, he saw the smooth surface of a boulder. He put his hands on the sides of the boulder and pushed into the soft earth around it until he felt the rock curve around behind itself. He planted his feet carefully and pulled with all his might. The boulder popped out of the ground. Thunder hoisted it up and cradled it against his shoulder. Another giant bent down and gathered up the earth Thunder had dislodged. He made a pile of it in his hands and began walking to the dam, right beside Thunder.

As Thunder walked, other giants passed him on their way to the quarry. He tried signing questions to them, but couldn't move his hands enough while holding onto the rock. The giants with free hands, those going in the other direction back to the quarry, were in cheerleading mode. *Good job!* they signed. *We're winning! Giants are supreme!* All of which was inspiring enough, but Thunder wanted an explanation. Why was the dam crumbling in the first place?

At the side of the dam stood Moon, one of the oldest giants on the plateau. Tattoos covered her from head to toe, and she was directing the giants carrying the boulders. She would point to the water side of the dam, or the land side, or the top, as each boulder-laden giant passed by. The giants obeyed her directions. Some giants waded into the river behind the dam—scattering the multitude of crows pecking at some dark objects on the water— and planted their boulders on that side. Others stepped onto the top of the dam and dropped their boulders there. Thunder saw the main overflow was almost shut off. The big river had swollen tremendously but it had not yet flooded any of the villages so the giants still had time to minimize the damage.

Apparently, though, the people of Dribbleton did not see it that way. They scrambled up the sides of the dam trying for higher ground. They must not come up to the plateau. With all the giants walking about, the pocket people would surely be crushed. Thunder's parents might be one of them. The people of Dribbleton did not like the giants and they would not do anything for them. Even so, they were still his people. They still deserved some consideration.

As Thunder approached Moon, she pointed left, which meant Thunder should go on the land side to place his boulder. He hesitated. The giant behind Thunder bumped into his back. Moon signed frantically. *What are you waiting for? Go.*

Thunder shook his head. He put the boulder down at his feet. *I can't go down that way,* he signed. *I'll step on them.*

They know better than to get underfoot, signed Moon. *We have to shore up the dam.*

My family is there.

Moon looked at him with annoyance. *Your family is here, Thunder. If you don't want to repair the dam, get out of the way for those who do.*

Thunder looked down at his boulder. Giants stepped around him and followed Moon's directions. They glanced at him with puzzled expressions. Thunder picked up his boulder and placed it at the edge of the cliff so giants who were directed to the gorge side of the dam would have to step over it. Pocket people looked up at him. *Go back,* he signed to them. *You are safer in your village.*

They screamed up at him. Thunder did not

know what they were saying. None of them knew sign language. No one in Dribbleton knew sign language. Oh yes, thought Thunder, you want nothing to do with giants, except you live on the big river, which would kill you all without the dam we giants built and maintain. *We're trying to help you,* signed Thunder, unable to think of anything else to do. *It's not safe for you here. You need to go back.* He made pushing motions with his hand, hoping they would understand they needed to get away from the dam.

Thunder felt a hand fall on his shoulder. He turned around. Stone stared at him.

I understand your concern, she signed. *But there's nothing we can do. They don't want to listen to us.*

Thunder's shoulders slumped. The pocket people from Dribbleton were still shouting up at him. He scanned their faces, to see if he could recognize any of them. He vaguely remembered a few from when he lived in Dribbleton. He wished they could recognize him. Then they would know he was trying to help. All the giants were trying to help.

Another giant picked up Thunder's boulder and wedged it into the dam. *Hey!* signed Thunder. *That was my boulder.*

Then why didn't you place it? What were you waiting for?

Thunder stepped away from the angry pocket

people of Dribbleton and pushed his chest into the other giant's chest. *It wasn't safe yet,* he said.

Stone tried to step between them. *The dam,* she signed. *We're here to save the dam, not fight.* Thunder saw her out of the corner of his eye. He kept eye contact with the other giant, the one who took his boulder. He wanted to pull away from this confrontation. He could not. The other giant's eyes were ablaze, wide and wild.

Stone grabbed his shoulder. Without thinking, Thunder put out his arm in reaction and accidentally caught Stone under her chin. Her head jerked to the side. She teetered, about to tip over. Her arms went up in an attempt to counterbalance herself, but she had passed the point of no return. She was going to fall.

Thunder forced his eyes away from the other giant. He looked wildly around for pocket people. They saw what was happening. Stone was about to fall directly on top of them. They ran in all directions.

Thunder somehow moved faster than he had ever moved before. He put out his arms, stepped quickly in Stone's direction, and managed to put himself between her and Dribbleton. She fell, but she fell against Thunder, avoiding a fall to the ground.

Thunder pushed her back up. She swatted at his

hands until he pulled them away.

What is the matter with you? she signed.

He took my boulder. Thunder looked around. The other giant was already gone. Probably back to the quarry to get another rock.

He was placing *your boulder. Like you should have been doing.*

Thunder felt miserable with failure. His shoulders slumped even more than before. *I know.*

Moon came striding up to Thunder. *We were doing fine until you got here,* she signed.

Even though she was clearly angry with Thunder, Stone quickly came to his defense. *The other guy was being rude,* she signed.

Rude? thought Thunder.

Moon looked at her? *Rude?* she signed.

Yeah, signed Stone. *Very rude.*

We don't have time for this, signed Moon. *Stone, go get more boulders.* Stone turned and began walking to the quarry. *Thunder, I want you on the water side of the dam. Scoop up the silt and mud from the bottom and shore up the boulders. Go!*

Thunder took in a deep breath. *What about Dribbleton? What about the pocket people?*

She pointed to a spot on the lip of the cliff. Thunder saw giants gouging out a large area with the ends of felled trees. Other giants placed boulders around the clearing so the Dribbletonians had an enclosure to keep them safe. Still other giants dragged a tree up the slope of the cliff wall in an S shape, making a path for the pocket people, who now swarmed to the path and started walking up it.

See? signed Moon. *You're not the only one who cares about them. We'll let them stay as long as they want. As soon as they see the dam is secure, they'll return to Dribbleton. Now get going to your assignment.*

Thunder thanked Moon and began to trudge around the end of the dam to the water side. The plateau all around here was now a giant mud pile. Thunder slogged through it with heavy steps. Great slabs of mud clung to his feet. While he had squabbled with the other giant, the rest of the giants had closed up the dam. The great mass of water from the big river was once again held back, but some spots on the dam still sprouted little streams where trickles of water got through. The procession from the quarry did not let up. They still needed to build the dam up higher, as a safety measure.

Thunder waded into the water. The crows opened their beaks and called out. Thunder scooped up a handful of mud from the bottom of the river and pushed it into the crevice between two large rocks. The mud was both sandy and silty. He scooped up more handfuls, filling gaps where he found them. As he worked, he was oblivious to anything else around him. He reached back and brushed against a clump of something soft, mushy like a rotten animal. A chill went up his spine. He turned his head and looked at what he had touched.

Bright flashes of light circled his vision, like iridescent crows. The palm of his hand held a dead pocket person, a child, one who had been dead for a long time.

Thunder made himself look up from the sight, as much to tear himself from the image of the dead child as to see what else was going on. Now he saw what the crows had been pecking at. The water held many dark shapes, some at the bottom, some partially submerged, some floating and collecting on this side of the dam. The shapes extended up the river and out of sight, all the way to the mountain, for all Thunder knew. They were pocket people. The river had risen behind the dam, and with it came hundreds of dead pocket people, down from the mountains to here, where they were collecting and where the crows fed on them like the happy opportunistic scavengers they were.

firefly

Firefly looked wildly toward the edge of the cliff. The giants would not tread there. One misstep and they could fall. So the edge of the cliff was the safest place to be. But with their pounding feet approaching rapidly, she could not get to the cliff in time. A tension born of fear gripped her throat. If she could not get to the cliff, she was in serious trouble. She could not stay here in the path of the giants. She would surely be crushed by one of their feet. *Sideways thinking. I think I need to get out of the way, but maybe the answer is the opposite.*

Firefly ran a few short steps off the flat path toward the approaching giants. A large rock stood nearby. Small to the giants, but large by her standards. Maybe it would be big enough. It was embedded in the ground on a slight slope. It had moss on the side and top, so it must have been there for a long time. It should be solid enough. She curled up on the ground next to the rock and tried to make herself into as tiny a ball as possible. The rock shook and trembled. In no time the feet of the giants were all around her, falling like enormous hail stones, if hail was the size of gorge houses. The rock beside her trembled and vibrated. The giants passed quickly and avoided the rock, exactly as she had hoped they would.

When the ground was still again, Firefly emerged from behind the rock and ran back to the path. The giants had obscured the footprints she had been following, but she continued on the path away from the cliff and found the tracks again. She ran for a few minutes and soon came to some algae hanging from large racks. How strange, she thought. Why would they put algae on racks like this? She kept going and came to the biggest door she had ever seen in her life, taller than the trees around her. It was made of logs stacked one on top of the other and it was wide open. She ran inside. A table and some chairs towered above her. Above *that* the cave's ceiling arched so high it wavered in her vision. She stood in the doorway and tried to catch her breath. Firefly called for her mother several times. No answer. She looked around the cave. Except for its enormous size, and for its being a cave, this space looked like a completely normal place for a person to live. She saw a cupboard and counter along one wall, a bed in a corner, and a chair next to a fireplace on the other wall. It was more sparsely decorated than most gorge houses. A giant bowl lay on the floor. This gave Firefly an instant scare. Was the bowl there to hold pet food? Did the giants have giant dogs or cats? She had never heard of such a thing, but who knew? Most people did not come up here, so how could anyone know?

She looked around, warily, approached the bowl, stood on tiptoe, and peeked over the edge. Empty. Wait. Not quite empty. She saw an ink stain on one side, near the top. It was a type of stain her own house had on some of the door handles and some of the walls. Even a few of the chairs. It came from her mother, who always had ink somewhere on her clothes or arms or face from when she tattooed the giants. Firefly liked seeing the stains in her house, it reminded her that she was part of an inking family and that someday *she* might be an inker.

Firefly walked around the bowl to examine the stain. She hoisted herself up on the rim so she balanced on her belly and put her finger on the stain. Yup. Still a little tacky. Not wet, but not completely dry. Her mother had been here not too long ago. Firefly let herself drop back to the floor. She felt her heart going like mad. She had never had so many heartbeats so quickly as she had these last couple of hours.

The giant must have tried to keep her mother trapped in the bowl, but somehow she escaped. She got the door open—Firefly was mystified as to how such a small person could open such a huge door, but her mother was an amazing person so she must have found a way—and she had escaped the giant's cave. Where would her mother have gone? Back down the cliff, of course. Maybe she climbed down the vine? But wouldn't Firefly have seen her on the vine? Maybe there were other vines on the cliff. Firefly didn't know what to do next. Should she try to find her mother or go back down or wait here for her? What would Mr. Epiderm advise?

She retreated from the bowl and went back to the open door and thought about where her mother would have gone to. Why had the giant put the bowl down on the floor? If he wanted to keep her mother trapped, he would have put her high up where she couldn't have gotten down. The bowl looked so inviting. It was like a little house of its own. Much cozier than being here, on the floor of the giant house, with all that room spreading out around her to forever. Firefly put her arms around herself and shivered. She had to make a decision but didn't know how to make the right one.

She heard some rustling in the woods. She gasped and turned around. A shape moved toward the cave. Firefly retreated behind the edge of the doorway so it hid her and she poked her head around a little to try to catch a glimpse of who or what it was. It was not a giant. It was some person or animal her size. Please let it be my mother, thought Firefly fervently. Please let it be Mom.

The shape became a person who stepped out of the woods and stood in plain view and looked around. Firefly came out from behind the door.

"Mushroom!" she said. "What are you doing here?"

"Firefly!" shouted Mushroom and ran toward her. He looked like he was in pain.

"What are you *doing* here?" said Firefly. She noticed bright burns reddening Mushroom's arms and legs. He must have come up on the vines. She still had some chunks of the nest in her pocket. She handed them to Mushroom and told him to apply it to the red areas. As he did so, his face registered relief.

"Thanks," he said.

"You're welcome. What are you doing here?"

"Did you find your mother?" said Mushroom. He looked past Firefly to the giant's cave. "Wow," he said. "This is big."

"Of course it's big," said Firefly. "It's a giant's cave."

"I know, but. Man. It is *big*."

"OK, Mushroom," said Firefly. "We've established that this cave is big. Now *what* are you doing here?"

"The dam sprung a leak," said Mushroom.

"I know," said Firefly. "The giants are fixing it. I saw it from the vines and I almost got trampled by some giants going there."

"So you know. Where's your Mom?"

"I don't know. She was here, but she's gone now."

"We have to get back to the gorge. Mr. Epiderm says we all have to get into boats and sail down the river to the sea."

"What?" said Firefly. "We can't live in the sea."

Mushroom shook his head. "Not to live. Not forever. Just until the thing with the dam is settled. The water is still rising behind the dam, Firefly. Even if the giants fix it today, it won't last. More water is coming. That's always been the plan, Firefly. If the dam breaks, we go to the sea. We have to find your Mom and get out of here."

As Mushroom spoke, some instinct in Firefly turned over on itself. She had always been afraid of coming up here to the plateau. She thought the giants would step on her, or she would became an insane person, or wild creatures would eat her. None of that happened. She had a feeling living here with the giants would not be such a bad thing.

"I don't think we should go to the sea," said Firefly.

"We *have* to," said Mushroom. "Mr. Epiderm and a lot of the other elders are saying it's our best chance. We can't stay up here, Firefly. We can't."

"If the river is rising," said Firefly, "going to the sea won't help. We will never come back to the gorge. It'll be under water. We have to move up here."

Mushroom shook his head. "Most of the elders could not climb the vines the way we did. They have to go to the sea. Firefly, why won't you believe me? Why don't you believe Mr. Epiderm?"

Mushroom did have a point about the elders. Mr. Epiderm himself couldn't climb up the vines. Neither could a lot of the older people, even the ones who weren't crippled. They wouldn't have the strength. Also little babies couldn't climb. And a lot of young children. A lot of people would need help, but that didn't matter. The rest of the gorge would have to find a way to get them up here. Maybe they could all climb up by Dribbleton. Or the giants could carry them all up, like that one giant who carried Firefly's mother. They were just going to have to do it, one way or another.

"I can't leave without my mother," said Firefly. "I can't."

Mushroom sighed. "I'll help you look for her, but then we *have* to go down. They're getting the boats ready right now, Firefly."

Firefly didn't want to hear anymore about some ridiculous plan to go to the sea. None of the river people had ever been to the sea. Sea waves were big and strong enough to drown any boat the river people could ever build. And once they were there, what then? How would they get back up the river? And why would they want to? The gorge would be under water. Giants are strong, but they aren't strong enough to stop a river from rising. Why did Mr. Epiderm want everyone to go to the sea? Was he afraid? He didn't have to be. The plateau wasn't so bad at all. Was going to the sea a sideways thinking plan? Firefly tried to see it that way, but it made no sense to her. Staying up *here* was the real sideways thinking.

"Mushroom," she said. "It's time we stopped living in fear all the time. It hasn't gotten us anywhere."

"What are you talking about?" said Mushroom. "Do you know where your mother is?"

"No." She turned from Mushroom, cupped her hands to her mouth and started shouting as loud as she could. "MOM! MOM!" She turned in a slow circle twice, shouting constantly. She cupped her hands to her ears, what Mr. Epiderm had called "making deer ears" and turned around slowly, listening for any sound from the forest. Mushroom did the same.

After a few seconds he whispered: "Hear anything?"

"No," said Firefly.

They repeated the shouting and the turning. Still nothing from the forest. Firefly began to feel true fear. What happened to her mother? Where was she?

She ran around to the other side of the cave. Mushroom followed. They stood at the base of a hill with a slope gentle enough for them to climb easily. Firefly looked up the hill for any tracks that might be there. Maybe her mother climbed the hill? No. Why would she? She would go down the cliff, back home.

"I don't think she's here," said Firefly.

"Then where is she?" asked Mushroom.

Firefly bit her lip. Her teeth trembled, bouncing up and down on her lip. Her chest thumped like mad. Why was her heart going so fast? Mushroom's face darkened. A shadow slid over them both. Mushroom looked up. It wasn't her heart. Her teeth were chattering because the ground was shaking. A giant was nearby. Firefly saw her, looming high in the treetops. She looked down at Firefly and Mushroom. Mushroom began running. "Let's get out of here," he said.

"Stop it," said Firefly. "They aren't trying to hurt us." The giant began to lower a net over them. Firefly saw it too late. A great wooden hoop encircled her in an instant. She crouched. A mesh of vines followed and slapped sharply against her back. This was how the giants trapped and killed animals. Firefly covered her head with one hand and reached out to Mushroom with the other, but he had escaped and was running as fast as he could into the forest.

Firefly peeked out from under her arm and saw Mushroom's feet receding rapidly. "Get help," shouted Firefly. "Don't let me die here."

Firefly dared to look up. The giant had a wide grin on her face and licked her lips. She moved her hand over the net covering Firefly.

THUNDER

Thunder waded out along the shore behind the dam where many of the floating bodies clumped together. He swept his arms out in front of him to scatter the crows and keep them from pecking at the bodies. The bodies were partially decomposed and mostly unclothed, though some had bits of rags, remnants of trousers and shirts, wrapped around their arms and legs. Some of the bodies were little more than bones, others had loose bits of flesh hanging from them. Pieces of ice still clung to many of them. As the ice melted, the bodies sunk below the surface. Thunder saw their grey and watery shapes collecting at the wall of the dam.

Thunder knew he was no great brain. He understood himself to be a brute force giant, as was most of his kind, but it didn't take much brain power to realize these bodies must have come from the glacier way upstream. The glacier was obviously melting, raising the water level in the river. And with that melting came a great many dead pocket people, perhaps an entire village or more.

Stone came and stood beside him. She moved her hands up. *We didn't want the pocket people to see this,* she signed.

Are they more calm now? signed Thunder.

A little bit. Still angry, but willing to wait for the dam to be fixed. Some are retreating. I think they want to go down to the sea.

The sea?

They think it's safer there.

But we're fixing the dam, signed Thunder.

Stone shrugged. *They have their own ways, the pocket people.*

Thunder nodded. He knew he thought differently now than when he was small. He was not as nimble or as imaginative now. Life for him, as for many giants, was simple. You eat, you sleep, you roam the woods. The world is a mystery, and that is an acceptable state of being. The pocket people were different, always thinking up new ways to do things, negotiating the tricky business of human relationships, probing the secrets of nature. Always asking questions. Giants didn't usually do those things. The prospects of a long life probably had a lot to do with that. He had lots of days ahead of him, so he could afford to be detached about calamitous events. Not so the pocket people. Their lives burned fast and bright. They couldn't risk losing a second of it.

I'm going to sit for a while, signed Stone. *Take a little rest. I'm tired and we're just mopping up now anyway.*

OK, signed Thunder. *It is better to keep the pocket people on the other side of the dam, isn't it?* He pointed at the bodies in the river. *They don't need to see any of this.*

Stone nodded. *No one does,* she signed. If these bodies were indeed the ancestors of the pocket people, some of them might easily be the ancestors of Thunder. This thought gave him an ache in his heart, exactly where the itch had been this morning.

Some crows descended on the bodies and dipped their beaks into the flesh and pulled up rancid hunks of it. Thunder put his hands in the water and pushed waves toward the crows, scattering them into the air. You make me sick, thought Thunder, the words so vivid in his mind he thought he said them out loud.

Some giants arrived on the shore with nets. They elbowed past Thunder and dipped their nets into the river. They lifted up the dead pocket people, swung around, and carried them back toward the quarry.

What's going on? he signed.

They're burying them, signed Stone. *Do you want to help? We have more nets.*

I have to get back to my cave, signed Thunder.

Oh.

Yeah. Important stuff.

Stone looked puzzled. *You have something important to do at your cave?*

Thunder hesitated. *It's complicated,* he signed. *There's a pocket person there.*

Stone's eyes went wide. *Oh. Really?*

Yeah, signed Thunder. *Are you going to stay here and help?*

I think I should. Come back if you can. We'll be here a while still.

Thunder turned from the river. The dam was still overrun by giants, most of them now in a more subdued mood as the bulk of the work on the dam was done and they were simply making sure every little crack and crevice was sealed tight. The top of the dam now stood a couple of feet above the level of the plateau. Thunder estimated the water's surface was only about twenty feet below the plateau on the upstream side, where the bodies of the ancient pocket people kept piling up. If the river rose only a little more than twenty feet, it would begin to flood the plateau. The water would not have to go over the dam then. It could simply go around it. The gorge would truly be doomed, and if the water kept on rising, the giants would also have to move away. They could not live in a lake. They might have to journey upstream and become mountain giants.

Thunder began walking back to his cave. It would be a hard thing to leave the plateau and the pocket people. He would not want to live in the mountains. It would be too cold, and algae would be scarce. Would they find game to catch for the pocket people? Who knew? Stone said some of the pocket people were going to the sea. They might drift there for a long time and end up somewhere else. An island, maybe. Or into some other gorge with another big river where they could re-establish their way of life.

Thunder was lost in his own musings, trying to come to terms with the changes coming, and did not at first notice Fern on the slight rise next to him, overlooking the dam. Her shape registered as a tiny object in his peripheral vision. He was about to walk by her when he noticed, almost as an afterthought, she was a person and she was shouting at him. Shouting at him? He was deaf. Why would she be shouting at him?

She signed: *Thunder. What. Is. Going. On?* She pointed to the procession of giants with nets over their shoulders, each of the nets dripping with piles of horrible wet *somethings*.

I didn't want you to see that, signed Thunder. *Why aren't you back at the cave? It's safer there. We are too many giants here. You could get stepped on.*

Fern's face was red. Her eyes were bright with fear or anger, Thunder couldn't tell which. Maybe both. Thunder had never seen her like this. Or any pocket person, for that matter. *Is that what happened to them? Did you step on them? You giants?*

Thunder hardly believed she was asking the question, as though crushing pocket people was something the giants would ever want to do. *No no,* he signed. *They died a long time ago. The glacier is melting, Fern.*

She looked at Thunder, at the other giants carrying the nets, and then back to Thunder. *The glacier?*

It's where they're coming from. They were trapped in it and now it's melting.

Fern shook her head. *Why would the glacier be melting?*

I don't know.

I never heard of river people being in the glacier.

Me neither, signed Thunder, *but it looks like we were wrong.*

That can't be, signed Fern. *We never lived in the mountains.*

That's what we thought, signed Thunder, *but it*

looks like we thought wrong. Fern frowned. *We're burying them,* signed Thunder. *It's what we do. We try to take care of you.*

Those people don't look taken care of.

They died a long time ago. Don't you understand? We're only burying them. That's all. We had nothing to do with their deaths.

Thunder made sure he didn't approach her. She was scared and unsure of him, which was completely understandable. She had never been up on the plateau before. She was right to be suspicious of what she saw. When he first came to the plateau, after he began to be giant, he was suspicious of everything. The trees, the animals, the food, and the giants. Especially the giants. They were so *big*. And clumsy. When he was a pocket person, he heard stories. How the giants ate the pocket people on purpose, which was bad enough in the eyes of his fellow Dribbletonians, but also how the giants were so clumsy they didn't see the pocket people and would step on them by accident, which was even more horrible, because accidents could not be planned for. Nevertheless, despite a lifetime up to then of being suspicious of giants, he eventually came to understand them as deeply benign, wanting only the best for the pocket people.

Fern retreated from him until her back touched a tree behind her. She stopped. *You mean you killed them a long time ago?*

Thunder slapped his forehead. Fern cringed. *No,* signed Thunder. *That's not what I'm saying at all. We don't kill pocket people. We love you all. We were you once. Here, get into my pocket and I'll take you there. I'll show you.*

Thunder took a step forward, which was the wrong thing to do. He had thoroughly underestimated how upset Fern was. She bolted and ran. She shot like lightning between Thunder's feet, flashing by the firefly tattoo on his ankle, and kept going in the direction of the cliff edge. Thunder cursed his own foolishness and instantly wished he could take the step back. He wanted to stop her. How could he without hurting her? She must not think he and the other giants were horrible monsters.

Thunder twisted around, pivoting on his hip, to try to catch a glimpse of her and see exactly where she was going. The force of the twist dislodged one of his feet from the ground and sent it against a tree, which made his knee bend wrong, which sent a jolt of pain up his thigh, which made him crouch over, which tipped his balance in the wrong direction, which sent him falling.

A giant takes a long time to fall, which usually gives him an opportunity to arrange things so the fall will not be too damaging. A giant could break anything in a fall: leg, knee, arm, or hand. Nothing worse than a giant with a broken hand. He could hardly carry anything *and* he had to talk with only one hand, which was like talking in only half words. Thunder had the presence of mind to relax his muscles and fold his hands over his chest. Thus arranged against the inevitable, Thunder continued to fall.

As he went down he saw Fern still running. What a mistake it had been to bring her up here. His back brushed against the trees. Branches splintered. Bark scraped at his sides and his neck. The final contact with the ground sent tremors for miles around and Thunder's heart felt heavy. What distant calamities had he caused by shaking the ground as he fell?

firefly

The giant's hand descended over Firefly. It blocked the light so she was in almost complete darkness. Firefly was not a girl given to screaming, but in this case such behavior felt entirely appropriate. She opened her mouth and screamed about as loud as it was possible for anyone to scream.

Which had absolutely no effect on the giant, of course. Firefly curled up into as tight a ball as she could and kept on screaming. If the giant couldn't hear her, maybe her mother was close by and would come and—what? What could her mother or anyone do against the giants?

The giant holding the net knelt down and slipped her hand under the hoop. Firefly scrambled along the ground to get to the opposite side of the hoop. Its dry grain rasped against her back. This was how they killed elk and deer. They trapped the animal and crushed it with their fingers. The giant moved her hand closer to Firefly. Firefly pressed herself along the curve of the hoop, pushing her foot against the wood, trying to wedge herself under, but the hoop was held down too tightly. She saw gaps on either side of the giant's wrist where the hoop could not curl around her hand. The gaps weren't big by giant standards, but they were big enough for Firefly to slip through. Firefly got up on her hands and knees to ready herself for a sprint. The giant's hand was right in front of Firefly, only inches away from breaking her bones with the merest gesture of her fingers. Firefly eyed the gap, ready to spring, then reconsidered. Even if she got out through the gap, the giant still had the net, and could still easily catch her. Firefly looked up through the vine mesh to the giant's face. She sure *looked* like she was ready to kill something, so what was she waiting for?

It soon occurred to Firefly that this giant might not be particularly interested in Firefly's demise. The giant did not move her hand. She remained kneeling like a patient rabbit. Firefly relaxed her legs and arms and sat back on the ground. She signed up at the giant. *Take away the net.*

The giant nodded and lifted the hoop. The mesh rose with the hoop. The giant's hand remained on the ground in front of Firefly.

Do you know where my mother is? signed Firefly.

The giant lifted her hand and signed to Firefly. *I don't know your mother.*

The ground shuddered and bucked, sending Firefly's teeth knocking against each other. *What was that?* she signed.

Probably a giant falling, signed the giant.

Firefly knew it was not good for a giant to fall. They were too susceptible to injury. *Why is he falling?* signed Firefly.

I don't know. We all fall, sometimes.

That must be awful, signed Firefly.

The giant shrugged. *It happens. Some of us never get used to being giants.*

You had to get used to what you were? thought Firefly. How odd.

We are all working hard to fix the dam right now, signed the giant. *You should be in a safe place with other pocket people. I can take you there.*

Pocket people? Is that what the giants called the river people?

There is no safe place anymore, signed Firefly, remembering what she saw of the dam.

The giant frowned. *Some places are safer than others. Climb up on my hand.* She put her hand back on the ground, palm down.

Firefly considered the offer. She was suspicious of this giant, of *all* giants. And yet. The giant could have killed her at any time since finding her. All she had to do was pinch Firefly's neck between her thumb and forefinger and that would be the end of Firefly. Her brain said it was ok to go with this giant. Her instincts said it was foolish. Which to believe?

Firefly turned the dilemma over in her mind for a few more seconds, then walked forward, put her hands on the edge of the giant's hand where thick hairs were arrayed like rows of sprouts in a garden, and hoisted herself up onto the back of the giant's hand. She crawled to the middle and huddled there with her hands wrapped around her knees. The giant didn't move her hand. Instead, she indicated with her other hand that Firefly should stretch out. OK, thought Firefly. This giant has done this sort of thing before. She released her legs and lay down spread-eagled on the giant's hand. She put her cheek against the skin. It was softer than she had imagined it would be. She wondered what it would be like to stick needles into this skin and inject ink the way her mother did. Could she do it and do it well?

The forest tilted slightly left, then slightly right, then began dropping down out of view. Firefly's stomach suddenly wanted nothing more than to leap from her belly. Her heart felt like it was going to pop out of her chest. She hung on while the giant raised her hand until it was wedged up against her shoulder. Firefly was now at least fifty feet above the ground. Maybe even a little more. The giant held her hand steady and waited. Firefly was obviously supposed to walk off the giant's hand and step onto the shoulder of her shirt. *Is this how it's done?* thought Firefly. She found leather straps on the giant's shoulder. Was she supposed to hang onto them? She gingerly got up from her prone position to a crawling stance and went forward a short way. All the giant had to do was pull her hand away at the very moment Firefly was stepping from it onto the shoulder, and Firefly would fall a long way down. She told herself again that the giant could have killed her at any time, and he did not do so.

Firefly rose up on her feet and stood on the giant's hand. It was like standing on something rubbery. She carefully took one step forward, then another. Before she stepped completely off the hand, she grabbed one of the leather straps and hung onto it like she had hung onto the vine, and used it to help pull herself across the crevice formed between the giant's hand and her shoulder. Finally, she stood on the leather of the giant's shirt. An enormous ear lobe hung down beside Firefly. She put her hand on it. This brought her some comfort. Her heart calmed down a little. She began to feel like she was no longer in any real danger.

The giant started walking. The ride was bumpy. Firefly tightened her grip on the leather straps and sat down on the giant's shoulder. She still bounced up and down a little with each step, but she no longer felt as though she was going to fall off. Firefly felt secure enough to do a little sight seeing. She was higher than the tops of most of the trees. They spread out all around her for miles and miles, a vast covering, like green waves over all the land. Upstream from the big river she saw the mountains, white against the blue sky. Firefly had never seen such a sight in her life. The gorge was nothing like this. It had some beautiful spots, places she liked to go, like some of the sandy beaches along the big river, and a few woodsy areas, but the gorge boasted nothing like this magnificence. No wonder the giants lived up here. Who would not want to live in the middle of such glorious beauty?

The giant slowed her pace. Firefly looked down. She saw newly splintered trees, and among the yellow shards, a fallen giant, who must have been responsible for the tremors she felt a few minutes ago.

The giant carrying Firefly raised her hands to talk to the giant on the ground. *Are you ok?* she signed. *Why don't you get up?*

The giant on the ground looked up. *There's a pocket person around here. I don't want her to get hurt. I have to make sure she got away before I disturb anything else around here.*

That must be Mushroom, thought Firefly, or my mother. She jumped up and down and waved her hands, trying to catch the fallen giant's attention.

I think it's safe, signed her giant. *I don't think there are any others around. I've got one of my own to take care of.*

OK, signed the fallen giant. *I'll get up. Give me room.*

He rolled over on his side and knocked over several more trees. The giant carrying Firefly kept walking. Firefly kicked at her earlobe and scraped her fingernails across it, trying to get her attention, but the giant was oblivious. Firefly turned around on the giant's shoulder and watched the other giant shake off broken branches like they were pesky bugs, slowly get up on his knees, and begin to raise himself up. She signed to him desperately. *Did you see my mother? Where is she?* The giant was not looking in her direction and soon they were too far apart for him to be able to see her at all. Firefly sighed and turned to face forward. Soon the dam appeared in front of her. Firefly saw that it was bigger than before, rising up and over the level of the plateau. Off to the side a procession of giants with nets slung over their backs, each net holding something indistinct, made their plodding way into the woods. Must be cleaning up the site, she thought.

Her giant stopped near the edge of the plateau. Firefly looked down at the big river in the gorge, almost impossibly far away from where she stood. On the lip of the plateau, near the edge, she saw a group of river people inside a small circle made of large boulders. The giants must have placed those rocks to mark out a sanctuary for the river people. They all looked up at her. She waved. They didn't wave back. Firefly had no time to wonder why. Her giant put her hand up to her shoulder. Firefly stepped onto it and spread herself out for stability. The giant moved her hand steadily and slowly down to the group of river people, who moved to create a clearing for her hand. When the hand was on the ground, Firefly hopped off. The giant raised her hand, touched her forehead with a slight tap, turned, and walked away.

The river folk moved closer to her. She didn't recognize a single one. They must not be from Craddleton. At least thirty of them stood clustered around Firefly, each one studying her like she was a bug in their food. Firefly got the impression they thought she shouldn't be in the enclosure with them. She told herself such thoughts were silly, but she did feel tension in the air, like she should be wary.

"Hi," she said. "My name's Firefly."

"You're not one of us," said someone.

"Of course I am," said Firefly. "I'm your size. Have you seen my mother? Her name is Fern. She's an inker."

"We don't know any inkers," said a man in the back.

"Oh," said Firefly. "How about Mushroom. He's a friend of mine from Craddleton. I think he got lost up here, maybe. Like my mother."

"We don't know anyone from Craddleton and we don't have anything to do with giants."

"Oh," said Firefly. Now she understood these were river people from Dribbleton. They lived next to the dam in those sod houses. They ate the salmon that swam up the river to die at the foot of the dam. They never took any help from any of the giants.

"We was getting drowned out of our houses," said someone else. "We had to come up here while the cursed giants were fixing the dam."

Cursed giants? Firefly had never heard such a phrase. So it was true: the Dribbletonians truly did hate the giants.

"It looks like we can go back now," said Firefly. She pointed to the dam. "It's all fixed."

"It won't stay fixed for long," said another of the Dribbletonians. "The water will keep rising. We're going to go back down and get in boats and go out to sea."

"That's what my friend Mushroom said. But I have to find my mother."

"Here now," said another of the Dribbletonians. "What was your mother doing up here anyway?"

"I don't know," said Firefly. "I thought she got taken up here, but the giants don't want us up here. She *wanted* to be here."

"She wanted to? You all from Craddleton are crazy people, sticking things into the giants. If you left them alone they would go away. It's no wonder they want to keep us all for their pets."

Firefly blinked. Pets? "No," said Firefly. "We're not their pets at all. They love us. They want to take care of us. And they want the tattoos. It helps them."

"They have brought the curses on themselves," said one of the Dribbletonians, an old woman, who stepped forward and stood in front of Firefly. "You are a child still, so you don't know. But the giants were one of us once."

"Everyone knows that," said Firefly. "That's why they care for us."

"No!" The woman spoke sharply and very loud. "Once we took care of ourselves. We fished and hunted, we made our own houses. Now you all do disgusting things for the giants so they will give you food."

Firefly's head was spinning. How could anyone think these things? Applying tattoos was not disgusting. It was art. Making clothes for the giants was not disgusting. How could a whole village think these things? Her mother had often told her the people from Dribbleton were different, and not only because they refused to spend any time with the other river people.

"The giants look after us. They always have."

Someone pointed to the line of giants streaming away from the dam. "Now what do you think they have in those nets?"

Firefly tried to see. She could not tell for sure. "I don't know," she said.

"It's us. Dead ones. They's burying the people like us that they killed."

Firefly tried to take in the substance of what this Dribbletonian was saying to her. None of it would fit into her mind at all. She thought fleetingly of sideways thinking, but her heart, still beating rapidly, wouldn't let anything make sense. "All I want to do is find my mother," said Firefly.

The older woman took a step forward. "And what of your father?" she said.

"My father?"

"Yes. You look for your mother, but what do you know of your father?"

Firefly did not know her father. Her mother told

her he died before Firefly was born.

"My father is dead," she said.

The old woman laughed. "Is that what your family told you about my son? Is that what your mother said, that my son is dead? After she lured him away from his own town and his rightful family? Made him into something he was not? Is that what she told you?"

Firefly was certain the woman must be mad. What gibberish was she talking?

"I need to get out of here," she said.

"No," said the woman. "You need to know the truth. The giants are what happens to us when we dare to step out of our own true place. My son laid down with your mother. That is why he turned into a giant and came to live up here."

Firefly backed away from the woman. She wanted to run from this circle of boulders. She could see a fresh tear in the earth, going down to the gorge, along the dam. This is where they must have come up. She could go down the same way, through Dribbleton and along the river to Craddleton. She ached for the safety of her own village.

The woman stepped closer to Firefly. Firefly took a step back. She felt the hands of Dribbletonians on her back, supporting her and holding her in place. Her heart rate went mad. The woman got as close as she could. Firefly felt the woman's breath on her nose and cheeks. She smelled of fish.

"So," she said. "This is the granddaughter my son made with that girl from Craddleton, before he became one of the cursed ones himself."

THUNDER

The thing was, it felt good to be on the ground, even if it took a fall to do it. Thunder didn't want Fern to run away, but she was faster than him, and he supposed if she wanted to run he could do nothing about it without trapping her in a net. He would not do such a thing to her. That was how the giants caught game. It wouldn't be right to treat *any* pocket person like she was a deer, much less Fern.

He stared up at the sky past the tree tops. So peaceful. He pushed his arms to the sides to brush away some of the broken trees. The pocket people were right. Giants were terribly clumsy and dangerous creatures. Not that it was his fault. He didn't ask to become a giant. No one did. It just happened, despite what his family used to say about it being a curse on them. Thunder had never felt cursed. Bewildered and confused, yes, but not cursed. The worst part of it was how none of the river people could help him when he first began transitioning to a giant. He had to climb up on the plateau and fend for himself. Those were the loneliest times of his life. He came down to the gorge a few times and waited for Fern near the trees where they used to catch fireflies, but she never came to see him. After a few long nights of waiting, he got the idea. She didn't want to see him. Not that he blamed her. What possible future could she and he have?

Thunder liked the feel of the ground on his back. It was solid, like him. The ground wasn't going to go away. It might change, but it was always going to be there. Not so for the rest of the world. The river looked like it would continue to rise, so now the giants and the pocket people were going to have to remake their world together. Perhaps even re-negotiate their arrangements for mutual benefit.

He caught a glimpse of motion from the direction of his house. A giant was coming his way. Thunder suddenly felt embarrassed. It was generally not considered appropriate to be on the ground like this. Giants usually liked to be up on their feet doing things, even if it was nothing more than kicking down trees that got in the way.

It was too late to get up now. The giant approached. Thunder glanced up at her. He did not recognize her but saw on her shoulder a pocket person who must have escaped from the circle of stones the giants had made for the fleeing Dribbletonians. The giant was probably putting her back for her own safety. The pocket people were sometimes too inquisitive and energetic for their own good. With so many giants milling about the dam repair site, it was best to keep them all in one place.

Are you ok? signed the giant. *Why don't you get up?*

Thunder tried shrugging but couldn't make his shoulders work that way from his prone position. He did not want this giant and this pocket person to see him sprawled on the forest floor. He wished the giant would keep walking. *There's a pocket person around here,* he signed. *I don't want her to get hurt. I have to make sure she got away before I disturb anything else around here.*

The pocket person on the giant's shoulder seemed to think that was very funny. She jumped up and down and waved her hands like she was laughing. It's not like I fall like this *all* the time, thought Thunder. I'm sure you fall sometimes too, don't you, pocket person? so don't get all high and mighty about it. Thunder thought about rolling over and getting up, but didn't want the other giant to see him in such an awkward position. It was absurd to be ashamed by such things, but there it was. He could not help himself. And it was always an awkward situation, getting up from a fall in the woods.

I think it's safe, signed the giant. *I don't think there are any others around. I've got one of my own to take care of.*

OK, signed Thunder. *I'll get up. Give me room.*

The giant moved on. Thunder rolled his body over and felt splinters of trees press against his back and arms and shoulders. The other giant could have helped him by clearing away some of the trees, but she would have had to stick around longer and Thunder would be even more uncomfortable, so it was probably just as well. He got onto his knees, and scraped earth and piles of ferns as he maneuvered his enormous limbs. He pushed up against his feet with his legs, came off his knees and rose to a standing position, feet firmly planted on the ground.

He saw above the treetops and instantly the world felt right again. The trees went on forever, broken here and there by gaps where the giants had their caves, or a great circle of stones. He brushed off a few branches which clung to his shirt and pants. They fell to the forest floor. The giants at the dam were still hauling away the dead pocket people. He should be helping them. It was a gruesome but necessary job. They probably needed help digging the graves. Once that was done, he and the other giants could work on what to do about the end of the world.

As Thunder began walking he saw a streak of color shoot across the forest floor. He looked down. Another pocket person in the forest. They were everywhere today. This one was not Fern, though, as Thunder had hoped. This was a boy and he was not paying attention to where he was going. He was looking behind himself and ran smack into Thunder's foot. He fell on his backside and looked up at Thunder. His expression was a study in fear. He backed away from Thunder, dragging his butt on the ground and shuffling with his hands and feet.

What are you so afraid of? signed Thunder.

The boy stopped. Thunder smiled at him. *What's your name?* he signed.

Mushroom, signed the boy. *You don't want to eat me, do you?*

Thunder laughed. The boy held his hands over his ears. So, some of the pocket people could be jokesters when they wanted to be. *We don't eat pocket people,* signed Thunder. *You taste awful.*

The boy's look of terror softened a little. *Ha ha,* he signed.

Thunder laughed again. *However, since your name*

is Mushroom, maybe I should reconsider my rule against eating pocket people.

Very funny, signed Mushroom. *I'm looking for my friend.*

Who's your friend? signed Thunder.

Her name's Firefly. She came here after her mother but one of you giants caught her in a net and I don't knew where she took her.

Thunder blinked and felt like he might fall again. *Firefly is here?* he signed.

So you do know her? Where is she?

Thunder could hardly believe his eyes. That pocket person, the one on the giant's shoulder, must have been Firefly.

I think I know where she went. Get on my hand. Thunder kneeled. Mushroom's eyes went wide and it looked like he was getting ready to run. Thunder put his hand down on the ground. The boy stepped onto it and Thunder conveyed him to his shirt pocket. The boy jumped into the pocket. Thunder made rapid strides toward the stone enclosure. When he got closer he slowed his pace and surveyed the scene. The pocket people assembled there were all from Dribbleton. Would they recognize him? No, how could they? Did it matter? Thunder wanted to make himself believe it did not. He still felt a deep hurt whenever he thought about his family, who no longer wanted anything to do with him. It was easier to let them think he was just another giant, not someone who once lived among them.

Mushroom, his new passenger, looked over the top edge of Thunder's pocket. He waved down at the group and kicked excitedly against Thunder's shirt and pocket. He must have seen Firefly. Thunder looked down at the group. One girl stood in the center, with Dribbletonians clustered around her. This must not be a good situation for her. For Firefly. His daughter.

He went down on his knees and put out his hand. The Dribbletonians scattered like frightened ants. Most of them went back down the path the giants had dug for them. A few, including Firefly, stayed up in the circle of stones.

Thunder raised his hands. The few people in the circle tilted their heads up and looked at him. *Are you Firefly?* He signed. He stared directly at the girl in the center. The rest of the pocket people in the circle turned and looked at her.

I am Firefly, she signed. *Who are you?*

Thunder's eyes welled up. He blinked away tears. *I am your father,* he signed.

Firefly stared at him. *What nonsense,* she signed. *If you are my father then tell me where my mother is.*

Thunder hesitated. *She came to my house,* signed Thunder.

I know that.

She knew? How could she know? *She got scared,* signed Thunder. *She ran away from me. I don't know where she went.*

Firefly stared for several seconds longer. *What was she scared of?*

She saw something she didn't understand. I couldn't explain it to her.

Firefly hesitated for a few seconds. She pointed to Thunder's pocket where the boy was kicking his legs and pounding his hands. *Let him down*, she signed. Thunder certainly had no objection to that. Mushroom obviously wanted to be on the ground with Firefly. Fine, he would let him down. Firefly looked angry and frightened. What was she angry about? Thunder hadn't done anything to Fern. He would never. Thunder put his hand up to his pocket in an absentminded way, intending to create a platform for the boy to get on. He held his hand there for a couple of seconds and felt the boy's small hands grab for the edge of his.

Firefly backed away from the center of the boulders to the lip of the cliff. Thunder could not understand her fear. She wanted to get away from him, but she had no reason to fear anything. No reason at all.

Wait, signed Thunder, snatching his hand away from his pocket to form the word, then realizing, too late, what that meant to Mushroom, who was just beginning to gain purchase on the edge of Thunder's finger. He was almost free, with his knees at the top seam of Thunder's pocket.

Fifty feet of air separated Thunder's pocket from the ground. Thunder saw Mushroom soon after he began his descent, and cursed himself for his clumsiness. The boy's mouth was open wide. Thunder began to swing his hand back. He needed to catch him before he hit the ground. Needed to save this boy's life. Mushroom, rolled over on his back, twisted in the air, grabbed spasmodically at something, anything, a distant cloud, or the crescent moon, or even a giant's finger, anything to keep from hitting the ground.

firefly

"I'm not your granddaughter," said Firefly to the woman only inches from her face. "That's ridiculous. How could I be?"

"There's only one way for people to be related to each other, child," said the woman. "My name is Fin. I never wanted my son to take up with someone from Craddleton, but what's done is done. Your mother kept me and him from you and that's as it might be, but the truth is the truth."

Firefly never ate fish. No one in Craddleton ate fish. Fish came from the sea where all kinds of things lived which the people of Craddleton did not care for. Mysterious animals with odd shapes and strange lives. Some people said the sea held creatures which carried their skeletons on their backs, or had tentacles, or stuck themselves to rocks. The fish swam in from the sea and up the big river past Craddleton toward the dam. Mr. Epiderm said before the giants built the dam the fish went all the way up to the mountains, but now, with the dam in the way, they could get only as far as Dribbleton where they mated and laid their eggs as they died.

And where the people from Dribbleton would catch them for their dinners. When Mr. Epiderm first told Firefly this, she could scarcely believe it. The fish swimming up the river were nothing more than vermin, dirtying up the water and clogging the water wheels. How could anyone use them for food? Mr. Epiderm told her that throughout history people had devised many different ways to survive. No shame came from eating fish, even if the people of Craddleton did not care for it. At various times the eating of deer and elk was considered degenerate. And what of the giants, who ate little flesh of any kind?

Firefly tried to keep all this in mind as she stood in front of the woman who claimed to be her grandmother and who smelled of fish so strongly Firefly thought she was going to be sick from the stench of it. She needed her mother more than ever now, to tell this fish-eater how demented she truly was. Firefly's father died a long time ago. Her mother told her so. She told her many many times.

Fin stepped back and spat on the ground. "You don't believe me," she said.

"No," said Firefly. "I don't believe you."

"And what would I gain by lying?"

"I don't know."

"Nothing. I don't want to be related to you any more than you do to me. I'm not making my life better by claiming I'm your kin."

"Then why tell me?" said Firefly.

Fin spat again. The glob left a wet circle in the dust. "We're all going to the sea now," she said. "We'll need each other to survive. The time for secrets might be done."

As she spoke the last sentence the ground shook. Firefly and the Dribbletonians looked in the direction of the sound. A giant with a river person in his pocket walked toward them. This was the same giant Firefly had just seen on the forest floor. She squinted at the figure in the pocket. Was it? He waved and shouted down to her. "Firefly! Firefly!"

Firefly waved back. "Mushroom!" she called.

The giant suddenly dropped to his knees. Everyone in the enclosure was immediately startled. "He's going to kill us all," said one of the Dribbletonians. They scattered away from Firefly and Fin and moved toward the edge of the cliff.

"Better not stay, child," said Fin. "It isn't safe." Fin ran to the cliff. Some of them were waiting on the edge of the cliff. Others began hastily running down the path back to the gorge floor.

They're being ridiculous, thought Firefly. This giant didn't want to kill them. The giant lifted his hands. *Are you Firefly?* he signed.

Firefly's heart turned over on itself. She blinked and could not pull her eyes away from the giant. How did he know her name?

I am Firefly, she signed. *Who are you?*

I am your father.

Firefly's heart skipped a couple of beats. Her head felt cold. *What nonsense,* she signed, not at all sure it truly was nonsense. Not after what the Dribbleton woman had told her. *If you are my father,* she signed, *then tell me where my mother is.*

She came to my house, signed the giant.

A chill went up Firefly's spine. Her mother came to the plateau to see this giant. She came here because—because—why? Because he was her father? *I know that,* signed Firefly.

She got scared, signed the giant. *She ran away from me. I don't know where she went.*

Fin's words, that the giants wanted to kill them all, echoed in Firefly's brain. *What was she scared of?* signed Firefly.

She saw something she didn't understand. What did he mean? thought Firefly. Her mother understood everything. *I couldn't explain it to her,* signed the giant.

Of course not, thought Firefly. You're a giant.

What could you explain to a river person? She pointed at Mushroom, still waving at her in the giant's pocket. *Let him down*, she signed. Mushroom needed to be safe on the ground. The giant moved his hand up to the top edge of his pocket. Mushroom reached out from the giant's pocket and grabbed at the hand. "Careful," said Firefly. Then, her voice rising: "Mushroom, be careful." Firefly took a few steps back to get a better look at how Mushroom was going to get down. It all looked so precarious up there, but she told herself she had been in a similar situation. Everything would be fine. She kept backing away, unthinking, until she came to the top of the path leading down to the gorge. Suddenly the giant decided to get all upset. He pulled his hand away from the pocket. *Wait*, he signed.

Mushroom, suspended by nothing, grabbed for air, and tipped forward off the lip of the giant's pocket. Firefly screamed. "Mushrooooooom!" What was wrong with this giant? This giant who was supposed to be her father? Why had he done that?

Now Mushroom screamed. "Heeeeeelp!" The sound of his voice, permeated with fear and desperation, chilled Firefly's blood. Mushroom's legs kicked at air. His arms reached up. He was going to come crashing to the ground.

Firefly ran toward Mushroom. He kept falling. The giant moved his hand as quickly as he could to try to get under Mushroom. Firefly saw what the giant was doing. She also saw he was much too slow. His hand was still moving toward Mushroom when Mushroom hit one of the boulders which formed part of the circle of rocks ringing her and the Dribbletonians. Firefly heard the sound like a tree smashing into stone. Mushroom slipped off the boulder and landed crumpled on the ground. He didn't move. Firefly ran to him and kneeled beside him. Blood leaked from his nose and mouth. His eyes looked up at her. They were bright, but unseeing. Firefly heard a voice calling for help with long piercing cries and only gradually understood that voice to be her own. Mushroom's eyes clouded over. No sound came from him.

The shadow of the giant's hand moved over Mushroom and covered Firefly. Firefly put her own hands up to her cheeks. Her eyes were wide and her vision was blurring. How could this happen? How could Mushroom be dead?

One of the Dribbletonian women ran to Firefly and knelt beside her. She put her hand on Mushroom's neck and held it there for a few seconds. She looked at Firefly and wrapped her arm around Firefly's shoulder.

Firefly, still in shock, felt everything like it was

a distant memory, clouded with the fluff of time. This happened a long time ago. In fact, it never happened at all. That giant did not just kill Mushroom. No. Such a thing was impossible. Mushroom could not die so easily.

The Dribbletonian woman, still with one arm around Firefly, motioned with her other in the direction of the trail. Others came and picked up Mushroom and carried him away from Firefly, down the path to the gorge floor. Firefly noted all this activity in a gauzy stupor of her own making. The shadow of the giant's hand flickered around her. She looked up. The giant was signing something. *I'm so sorry. I'm so sorry.*

Firefly signed nothing in return. The giant backed away a few steps, turned, and walked away. He receded toward the dam. Other giants had stopped their activity and were staring in Firefly's direction. What were they looking at?

Oh, thought Firefly. Me. They are looking at me.

"Why?" she said aloud. "Why are they looking at me?"

The Dribbletonian said "I don't know. No one knows why the giants do what they do." She tried to pull away from Firefly. Firefly would not let her. She pushed herself into the embrace of the fish-eater.

After a long time, Firefly got to her feet and began walking back to the trail. She was vaguely aware of some emergency among the river people. It was unsafe to still be on the river, wasn't it? She asked the Dribbleton woman who walked with her.

"Don't worry" said the woman. "We'll take care of you this night. We still have some time before the river rises over the dam again. Tomorrow you can go back to your own people."

Firefly nodded, still in a doughy nowhere. The trail the giant's had dug for them was an infinite snake and they were crawling down its throat to an oblivion which Firefly could only welcome. To be swallowed up by a softness that blocked out the light would be the most welcome thing in the world right now. She took small steps. The ground under her feet was springy, like being on the giant's shoulder had felt earlier. She had been on a giant's shoulder, hadn't she? The giant tried to help her? Put her somewhere safe?

After walking for ages they came to a small village with narrow streets lined with houses made of grass and mud set far apart from each other. It was not something Firefly had expected of the Dribbletonians. She had always thought of them as living in awful little houses. Only these weren't awful at all. They looked as cozy as anything in

Craddleton. Firefly began to feel as though, perhaps, the world was not going to swallow her up after all. The woman beside her guided Firefly to a sod house off the river. Firefly saw nets, smaller versions of the one that trapped her on the plateau. They leaned against the side of the house. The people of Dribbleton must use these to catch their fish, she thought. Firefly went into the house. She still half expected it to be dank and smelly. Instead, she entered a room radiating a welcome warmth and comfort with a table in one corner and a fire smoldering lazily in a fireplace in another. She sat at the table and someone put a mug of broth in front of her. It smelled like fish. She didn't care. She sipped it and her disconnectedness instantly disappeared. The table, chair, and bowl all slotted into place with an almost audible snap, anchoring her to the rough ground. Her feet scuffed the floor as she swung her legs.

A plate of roasted squash and a wooden spoon appeared on the table in front of her. Firefly dug into it and put a small piece in her mouth. The flavor seeped into her being. This is what it was like to be loved, wasn't it? She was in Dribbleton, but she was safe and attended to.

"Where's my grandmother?" said Firefly.

"You mean Fin?" someone asked. Firefly looked around. Four women clustered next to her.

"Yes," said Firefly. "I mean Fin."

"She went to Craddleton," said one of the women. "She needs to find your friend's family. To tell them what happened."

Mushroom's family. Yes. They needed to know.

"Thank you for bringing me here," said Firefly.

"It's the least we could do after what that giant did to your friend."

"Where is Mushroom?"

The women exchanged pained looks. "He's in another house."

"Can I see him?"

"Oh, child," said one of the older women. "What's the point? You know he's died."

The word "died" felt like a stab through Firefly's heart. She would have to get used to this new world in which Mushroom was...not there.

"I know," said Firefly. "But he shouldn't be alone."

"He isn't," said the older woman. "We're taking care of him. We have someone with him."

"But not one of his own," said Firefly, scarcely believing she even said it.

The woman looked surprised, but only for an instant. "You're right," she said. "Come with me.

The woman went out the door. Firefly followed her down the street, past sod houses bustling with activity as Dribbletonians gathered up their belongings and hauled them to the shore of the river, where boats awaited.

"You're evacuating?" Firefly asked.

"Have to," said the woman. "The sea will be our home now. Yours too, I expect. I suppose it's the thing we need, finally, to be rid of the giants once and for all. In time I believe we—all the river people—will see this forced migration as a blessing in disguise."

They stopped at a house. The woman hesitated at the door. "You're coming out of your shock, now," she said. "So this might be hard for you. Are you ready?"

Firefly nodded. The woman opened the door. Firefly stepped in. Against the far wall Mushroom lay with a blanket covering him up to his chin. Dried fish tails covered his eyes. Firefly blinked. A familiar man sat in a chair next to him.

Mr. Epiderm rose up on his canes and stood unsteadily, a definite shake in his stance. "I'm so sorry," he said.

Firefly walked to him, fell against his shoulder, and wept with uncontrolled grief.

THUNDER

Thunder's hand was too slow. He moved as fast as he could, as any giant could, but the boy kept falling, hit a boulder, and slumped to the ground before Thunder could do anything about it. Firefly ran to her broken friend. Her mouth was open. She must be screaming, thought Thunder. She must be screaming for the world to fix her friend. Thunder wanted, with all his heart, for Mushroom to stand up, dust himself off, and walk away.

But Mushroom would never stand again. He had fallen much too far. Thunder reached out. He watched as the pocket people lifted up the boy and took him down to the gorge. Again, like a creature unwilling to learn, Thunder's hand moved forward. He wanted to help. Needed to fix what he had done.

Firefly looked up at him. She was gone from her body. He saw only her staring eyes, searing in their simple, unstated accusations. Thunder raised his hands. *I'm so sorry,* he signed. *I'm so sorry.*

No reply from Firefly. Thunder took a couple of steps backwards. A cold relief enveloped him.

He did not have to stay here. He did not have to be part of this grief. He was a giant who made a mistake. All giants made mistakes. And sometimes pocket people died. That was the way it had been since before anyone could remember and that was the way it would continue to be. In the meantime, the giants did what they could for the pocket people.

He turned from the enclosure and walked toward the dam. He had tasks still to perform. Other dead pocket people needed tending to. The giants, still laboring on the dam, stopped and stared at him. Stone was among them.

What happened? she signed.

A boy fell out of my pocket, signed Thunder.

Is he ok?

Thunder could hardly form the words. He still felt the boy's hands on his own hand. The gentle pressure was the personification of the trust the pocket people invested in the giants: *You are solid and benign. You will take care of me.*

Thunder shook his head. *He died,* he signed.

Stone looked shocked. *Are you sure?*

Thunder nodded.

Stone put her arm around Thunder's shoulder and guided him past the dam to a hill near the quarry. She had him sit down. He did so with difficulty. He only wanted to walk away from everything. The gorge, the dam, everything. His head hung down. He could not look up. Not now. Maybe not ever.

Stone put her hand under Thunder's chin and made him raise his head. *Do they know it was an accident?* she signed.

I don't know, signed Thunder. *I'm sure they must hate me now. Maybe they hate all of us.*

Forget about that, signed Stone. *We have to keep their trust, now more than ever. The dam will only hold for another couple of days at the most, then the worst flooding we've ever seen will come through the gorge. We need to move them out.*

Thunder looked past Stone to the base of the hill beyond. The giants had dug a massive pit and they had filled it with the bodies of the pocket people who had come down the river. Thunder rose from his sitting position and walked over to the pit. Already giants were pushing earth back into the pit, covering the skeletons and bodies of these ancient people. Stone followed him. Thunder was aware of her presence, and at the same time aware that her presence meant very little now. None of them meant anything much at all. The pocket people did not need the giants, except to bury them, and what good was that to a people?

Thunder, signed Stone. *Do you understand what I'm signing?*

Thunder fell to his knees and began pushing dirt into the pit. He worked methodically and with great power, feeling the weight of the broken world upon him. Here was the least he could do for them and for himself: take care of their dead.

Stone put her hand on his shoulder, and tried to make him turn around. Thunder shrugged her off. The other giants, who had been working on the burial, stopped moving earth and stood and stared at Thunder. He was conscious of their stares, and welcomed them.

Finally Stone grabbed him by the neck and pulled with all her strength. Thunder got yanked away from his task despite himself. He looked down at the ground. He had begun to dig up dirt from around the mass grave. He was breathing very hard, unable to stop taking in great mouthfuls of air.

What's wrong with you? signed Stone.

Nothing. I'm finished here. I need to go there. He pointed in the direction of the mountains.

What are you talking about?

I'm not safe to be around. I'm going to live in the mountains.

Stone shook her head vigorously. *No! The pocket people need us.*

Thunder stepped back from her. *The pocket people are going out to sea.*

Stone looked surprised. *The sea?*

Yes.

They'll drown. They're much too small. They'll drown in the sea.

Maybe so, signed Thunder. *That's no longer my problem.* He turned from Stone and began walking in the direction of the mountains.

Stone's hand grabbed at his shoulder. Thunder shook her off. Other giants moved aside to give him an open path. He did not look at any of them. Instead, he fixed his gaze on the mountain in the distance. It was gray in early twilight. He knew it was covered in white snow, and also knew it was a long distance away. It would take him hours to get there, which was exactly what he needed right now: a task that took a long time and did not require much thought.

He left the giants behind. He left the dam, the quarry, and the mass grave of the pocket people. Guilt gnawed at him. He should stay and help. An even deeper sense of relief buoyed him up. He was free of them. He didn't need to spend time with the pocket people or try to make their lives better. He only had to make his own life better.

Thunder came to a clearing. He stopped. He had been here before. This is where the giants had created a great circle of stones. Meetings were sometimes held here, when the giants had decisions to make. Such occasions were rare. Giants usually did not have a make a lot of decisions.

Some giants, especially the tattooed ones, liked to come here at other times and sit in the middle of the circle. They remained for a long time, savoring the peace. Others would come for a few short minutes. Thunder had added stones to the circle. Most giants had. It was now an enormous structure, much more than a single circle. There was a wide circle on the perimeter, and many circles in the interior. Some lined up with the sun and moon on solstices and equinoxes. Others were arranged in pleasing patterns that had nothing to do with the sky. Most were large boulders from the quarry, tilted up on their ends, and stuck into the ground.

The air was windless, as still as the mountain. Such a beautiful evening. The moon, a little past three quarter's full, hung in the sky and cast silvery light on the forest. How could the end of the world happen on such a day as this? How could Mushroom die on such a day as this? Thunder stepped forward and walked carefully past the outer circle and into the center of all the circles. He saw motion in the dying sunlight. Several deer and some elk. They looked in his direction, but did not look up. Even after centuries of living next to the giants, they could not make themselves believe there could possibly be creatures taller than the trees. He watched their dark outlines and their shiny eyes. Thunder took a small step toward the animals. They froze. Thunder stopped. He heard a rustle of branches from off to the side. Another giant was here. A hooped net fell from the sky. The animals bolted. Some escaped, but it was too late for most of them. They were trapped in the vine mesh. Thunder turned to see who was at the other end of the net. He stamped his foot. The hunter looked at him.

Moon, he signed. *Is that you?*

She looked at him. She put one foot on the handle of her net and stood up so she was at his eye level. *Thunder? Yup, it's me all right. Best time to catch these critters is now, when the fading light confuses them.*

Yes, signed Thunder. *Very true.*

And they're going to need them in the gorge. Have to get a lot of food ready if the pocket people are going to survive in the sea. She eased herself closer to the mesh. *Help me dispatch them, will you?*

Thunder stepped closer to the net. The deer were sprawled on the ground, kicking and trying to escape. The elk snorted and tossed their heads. He had killed many creatures like this for the pocket people. All it took was one squeeze of his hand, right at the neck, and they were finished.

Come on, signed Moon. *I can't hold them down and break their necks at the same time. Some will get away.*

Maybe we should let them, signed Thunder.

What? Don't be silly. Come help me.

You know the pocket people aren't coming back, don't you? signed Thunder.

Moon leaned closer to Thunder. The light was almost completely gone now, but the starshine lit up Moon's face enough for Thunder to see her expression: she looked thoroughly disgusted with him. *So you killed one of them. Are you going to let that doom them all?*

You know?

Of course I know. Everyone knows. That doesn't change our responsibility to them. Or yours.

Responsibility? Why do we have a responsibility to any of them? They can get along fine without any of us.

Moon sighed. *Do I have to get into this now?*

Into what? signed Thunder, irritated with her. Why did she love them so much? Why didn't the giants just leave them all alone?

Are you forgetting we were one of them once? signed Moon.

Of course not.

I do it to help my family.

You said your family is up here.

Moon shrugged. *That was to get you to do your job. Truth is, we have two families. The ones who created and raised us, the river people, and the ones we live with now. The giants.*

Maybe we aren't doing them any good, signed Thunder.

They would starve without us.

No they wouldn't. The people of Dribbleton don't starve.

Moon dropped her hands in an expression of exasperation. Thunder saw her tattoos in the star light, all up and down her arms and over her face and head. Every square inch of her was covered in tattoos. Moon raised her hands again. *I used to get the itch all the time,* she signed. *Sometimes everyday. I'd go down there for the inking. Once I fell. I ended up with my head in the big river.*

Thunder's hands twitched. What did any of this have to do with him?

My nose was under water, signed Moon. *I was going to drown. The inker saved my life.*

How? signed Thunder.

He used his hoses. He couldn't move me, but he could snake his hoses into my nostrils. That's what he did. Right there, on the spot, he came up with a trick to save my life. I owe them life, signed Moon. *I can't abandon them now.*

Fine, signed Thunder. *But I can't kill anything else today.*

Moon's face softened. *OK*, she signed. *I'll do it myself.*

Thunder watched her slide her feet along the handle toward the hoop. She bumped some of the stones in the circle with her knees. When she had slid all the way to the hoop she bent down and put her hands on one of the struggling deer. She twisted its neck efficiently and the dear went limp. Thunder looked away. A few minutes later Moon stood.

All done, she signed, *no thanks to you. Are you going to at least help me take these down?*

Thunder stepped forward. Moon lifted the net off the dead animals and began putting them onto the mesh. Thunder kneeled beside Moon and dropped some of the deer and elk into Moon's net. They were still warm and pliant. Thunder knew the pocket people were going to appreciate all this bounty.

Moon pushed the handle of the net towards Thunder. Thunder shook his head and stood up. *I can't go down there now,* he signed.

Moon dropped the net. *I would like to give you the time you need,* signed Moon. *But there* is *no time. The pocket people have to get ready to go out to their tempo-*

rary homes.

On the sea, signed Thunder.

Yes. On the sea.

They aren't coming back. The river is going to rise and drown the gorge. It's going to rise and drown us, our caves.

You are so pessimistic, said Moon. *We have a plan.*

What plan?

Moon handed him the handle of the mesh. Reluctantly, he took it and slung it over his shoulder so the dead animals hung behind him. There was enough here to feed all of Craddleton for a few days. It would be best to get them down to the gorge where the pocket people could skin and gut them and get them roasting on spits.

We're going to divert the flow of the river, signed Moon as they began walking back toward the cliff's edge. *We giants are all going to go up to the mountains and gouge out a path for the river that will take it away from the gorge and away from the plateau.*

Thunder looked at Moon like she was demented.

Believe it, signed Moon. *We're going to move the big river and you are going to help.*

firefly

Firefly pulled away from Mr. Epiderm. Her face was wet with tears.

"As soon as I heard the terrible news," said Mr. Epiderm, "I came right over."

Firefly could not look at Mushroom, lying on the table beside her. "How did you come?" she said.

"By boat. Many people are on the water right now. I hitched a ride with one of them."

Firefly wiped her cheeks and eyes. "Have you seen my mother?"

Mr. Epiderm looked startled. "Why no," he said. "You never found her?"

Firefly shook her head. "She was at the cave of the one who killed Mushroom. Mr. Epiderm, he's my father. The giant who killed Mushroom is my father. Did you know? Did you know my father is a giant?"

Mr. Epiderm turned pale.

Firefly blinked. Her mouth fell open. "You *did* know."

Mr. Epiderm shook his head. "No, Firefly. I thought it *might* be so, but I never knew for sure. Your mother would never say anything about your father, but I knew her when a young man from Dribbleton would come to town and court her. I think some of us in town thought he must be your father, but no one knew he became a giant."

"Wouldn't it have been obvious?" said Firefly. "He didn't stay around after I was born. Wouldn't that mean he was a giant?"

Mr. Epiderm shook his head vigorously. "I know it must seem obvious now, but your mother and this boy—they were from different towns, you see. The families could not get along. It was entirely natural that the boy should disappear once your mother became pregnant. It was the way his parents and your mother's parents would want it."

Firefly struggled to make all of this fit into the world she had known up to now, but it was impossible. The simple fact was her mother lied to her about where she came from, and that lie distorted everything in Firefly's world. "That's just great," said Firefly. "My mother lies to me all my life, and my father turns out to be a killer."

Mr. Epiderm's eyes widened. He shook his head. "No, no," he said. "Surely Mushroom's death is an accident. No giant would purposely kill a river person. Never."

"OK," said Firefly. "How about this: My mother lies to me, and my father turns out to be a clumsy and deadly lummox. Also deformed. Is that better? My grandmother said the giants are cursed. I think she may be right about that."

One of the Dribbleton women put her arm around Firefly. "You shouldn't listen to such talk right now," she said.

"Maybe so," said Firefly. "All I know is my father killed my best friend."

The woman clucked her tongue. "It might be best for you to put your hard feelings away long enough to mourn your friend, don't you think?"

Firefly looked into the woman's eyes. She was so kind and understanding. How could the people of Craddleton have hated the people of Dribbleton for all these years? This was a *good* person who was trying to help her feel better. Firefly leaned closer. The Dribbleton woman's soft skin had the odor of fish about it, but Firefly was beginning to like the smell of fish. Its power cut through everything else. And the woman's firm arm around Firefly's shoulder was enough to anchor Firefly to the ground. She was still angry with her mother and with her father—such a foreign concept: *father*; one she would have to get used to—but this fish-eater, this Dribbleton woman, was right. There would be time for answers later. She took a deep breath and let it out slowly. Her body still trembled with grief. "There, there, child," said the woman. "We'll bury him now. Remember him later."

Firefly nodded. Bury him now, she thought. Remember him later.

The house shuddered. Mr. Epiderm looked up.

"Giants," whispered Firefly.

The Dribbleton woman released her. The house shuddered again. And again.

"What are giants doing in the gorge after sunset?" said Mr. Epiderm. "I think maybe they must be going a little mad on the plateau."

"No maybe about it," said Firefly.

They went to the front door and looked down the street and across the town to the cliff, silvery in the darkness. Firefly saw a large indistinct shape moving far in the distance. A giant coming down the path. Upon seeing him, Firefly felt only rage. If she had a good club at hand, even a small one, she half believed she would run down the streets of Dribbleton and kill the giant. They were so clumsy and stupid, the best thing for them was to have all their bones broken. If they were all lying dead on the ground they could never do any damage ever again. There would be peace in the gorge and in her own heart. Firefly's face grew warm with the thought of it. Her whole head became hot and the night took on a reddish tint. How could she have ever wanted to do anything for any of them?

She heard Dribbletonians calling out, but their cries were incoherent. She could not understand them. The giant—she could not tell, in the darkness, if it was her father or not—came to the edge of town, bent down on one knee, and dropped a dark heap of something on the ground. He rose, looked at the town for a few seconds, turned and began climbing up the cliff.

"What on Earth?" said Mr. Epiderm.

Firefly bolted from the doorway and ran down the street. The Dribbletonians watched her go by from their houses. She came to the edge of town and saw what the giant had left: several deer and elk. Gifts, she supposed. Her father trying to make amends by offering food?

Firefly knelt and put her hand against the belly of one of the deer. It was still warm. So, it was not only food, but fresh food. He killed it recently, probably within the hour. The tepid blood beneath the deer's fur and skin still offered some pulse of life in a perverted way. The river people could butcher this creature and roast it and eat it. It would give them sustenance for their migration. This was the ancient understanding between the river people and the giants. They offered food—life—in exchange for vital services to the giants. In years past Firefly would have been happy to butcher and eat this deer. She had helped her mother prepare and roast many of them. Not tonight. Not this deer. She stood.

"I do not disrespect your life," she whispered to the deer. Then, louder, wanting the entire gorge to hear her: "I do not disrespect the life of these deer and these elk, but I do not accept this gift from the giants."

She ran after the shadow, gray and indistinct in the distance. It was already far up the cliff. Firefly ran anyway, as fast as her legs could carry her. Her breath came in gasps. Her head felt hot and full. They could not make her feel better or calm her anger with food. She ran blindly. She felt the dam beside her, a *presence* in the night, like a being from some other realm. She stopped and took in breaths in great gasps. She spat on the ground. She felt as though she were poised between two worlds. The dam was the skin between them, a fragile layer of rock completely inadequate against the rising river. No one had power against that. Not even the giants.

Firefly took a few steps off the path and sat next to the dam. She put her hand on one of the boulders. Giants carried these like they were pine cones. They built this dam for the river people, yet any giant could crush any river person to death with stunning ease. Why did Mushroom follow her up the plateau? Everything would have been different if he had stayed down where he belonged. If *she* had stayed down. Or if her mother had stayed down. If if if. No calamity can be undone with ifs. What happened is what happened. Firefly put her ear to the boulder. She wanted to hear the river. She wanted to listen to the mountains. Didn't they speak to the river people by water? Didn't the truth of the mountains and their past come to them in the current which the dam regulated and tamed? As if the past needed taming.

The boulder had nothing to say. Mr. Epiderm had explained to her once, in one of her lessons, how the boulders the giants used to build the dam had been pushed down from the mountain by vast glaciers many years ago. They must have stories to tell about their journey from the mountain down to here. This one was quiet and inert. She looked up towards the top of the dam. The crest was lost in the darkness. Tiny deposits of reflective rock sparkled on the boulders. Their patterns mimicked the stars arrayed behind them.

Was that the answer? The rocks were the stars? And what were the stars? What did they have to say to her?

She listened. Heard mostly her own heart beats,

the blood in her ears. Eventually that roar subsided and she heard only the eternal rush of water filling the gorge.

She turned to go back to Dribbleton. No running this time. She walked slowly. The people there, those who remained, stood outside their homes and watched her. They mostly nodded their approval and some reached out to touch her as she went by. She knew none of them would take the deer either. The giants must know this too. Why did they waste their time bringing the deer to Dribbleton?

As she neared the house where Mushroom still lay, she heard Mr. Epiderm's voice. He was singing *that* song.

In morning light,
my heart's delight,

is slinking in
and inking skin.

To draw the fire
of your heart's desire;

to break your bones
and hear your moans.

Inside the house, Dribbletonians held candles and bowed their heads. Mr. Epiderm sang the song over and over, as though he was delivering Mushroom to a deep sleep. Firefly went into the house and stood behind the group. Mushroom's parents stood weeping and humming the song. The river people were coming together now. People from Craddleton attending a memorial for one of their children in Dribbleton. Such a thing would have been unthinkable even yesterday.

Such comfort in a few lines of verse and a simple melody. It tied them together. They had all heard the song as children, and the grownups, as they became parents, sang the song to their children, and so on. Mushroom's parents held each other. Firefly saw his mother's hand wrapped around his father's hand, both turning white from the strain. They trembled. Their voices worked hard not to falter as they sang the lullaby. Firefly could not look at them for long. It was as though she knew she should not witness something so private. They rocked back and forth on their feet, lost in the sound of the song. The melody was like the river, in a way: flowing serenely and quietly, always repeating, never ending. Delicate as frost, but sustaining in its simplicity and perseverance.

Near the front of the throng, right next to Mushroom, Firefly saw her grandmother. Her grandmother! Fin. A fish-eater. A person born and raised in Dribbleton. Her head was bowed and she sang the song too, even though she knew nothing of inkers.

Firefly remained at the back of the room for several more minutes. She began to feel lost, as if she was again a foreigner in this house, this town. The heat from the people and the candles became stifling. She was about to step outside when Mr. Epiderm stopped his singing. Everyone else stopped humming. The silence was filled with the fullness of meaning she had wanted from the boulder but did not receive.

Fin stepped back and gave Mushroom's parents a blanket made of river reeds, the kind Mr. Epiderm used to make his paper. Mushroom's mother and father draped the blanket over Mushroom. Other Dribbletonians helped them wrap Mushroom. They lifted him off the platform. The rest of the assembled people parted for them as they carried Mushroom slowly through the room, toward the door. They passed Firefly. She tried to see Mushroom's mother's face, but her head was down. Mushroom's father looked straight ahead. His jaw was set hard.

The Dribbletonians followed them outside and stood next to Firefly in a single file. Mr. Epiderm remained behind. "Where are they taking him?"

said Firefly.

"To the cemetery," said Mr. Epiderm.

"They can't wait to bury him?"

"It's best to do this quickly," said Mr. Epiderm. "We have to leave the gorge. The river is rising. We can't stay here any longer."

"I thought we still had a couple of days."

"Maybe," said Mr. Epiderm. "But this is not something we want to risk being wrong about."

Firefly nodded. Her world, her gorge, was going to disappear. The thought left her with such a feeling of isolation and dread she could barely make herself think about it.

"I still don't know where my mother is," said Firefly.

"We will have to trust she found her way onto a boat. She may be on her way to the sea right now."

"She wouldn't go without me."

Mr. Epiderm nodded. "Not out of choice," he said. "But she would assume you'd found a way as well. And she'd be right."

"Have you been to the sea before?" said Firefly.

Mr. Epiderm shook his head. "Never."

"It's supposed to be scary, isn't it?"

"I've heard stories, but stories are often exaggerations."

"That song you sang."

"Yes," said Mr. Epiderm.

"I want to do that. I want to break their bones. All of them. I want to hear them moaning."

"You should go to the graveside, now, Firefly. You need to say goodbye to Mushroom."

"He broke Mushroom's bones, Mr. Epiderm. He broke him. He broke him so he died without saying anything. No moans. No words. Nothing."

Mr. Epiderm stopped trying to make her feel better. He nodded. "I know," he said. "It's horrible. But you should go, Firefly. You need to."

As he spoke, his eyebrows lifted in a jolt. His mouth fell open. "Fern," he said.

Firefly turned around. Her mother stood in the doorway.

"You need to come with me now," she said to Firefly. "Up to the plateau and onto the mountains. That's where we came from. That's where we need to go back."

THUNDER

The weight of the net handle dug into Thunder's shoulder. The load wasn't too heavy for him, but it always felt like creatures weighed more dead than alive.

We are only giants, signed Thunder to Moon. *How can we move mountains?*

Moon shook her head vigorously. *Look carefully at my hands,* signed Moon. *Not mountains. The river.*

Oh, signed Thunder. *That makes so much more sense.*

Sarcasm is not productive, signed Moon.

Neither are fantasy schemes with no hope of success.

How can you be so ignorant of your own history? signed Moon.

Now you're going to tell me giants have a history of redirecting rivers.

Moon turned her back to Thunder and pulled off her shirt. Her tattoos gleamed in the odd half light around them. Thunder had never seen so many tattoos in one place. He had always known Moon was covered with them, but even giants with full coverage rarely displayed them like this.

Moon held her hands above her head. *Start at the top left,* she signed. *Read down.*

Thunder examined the image on Moon's left shoulder blade. It depicted a flood. Dark clouds hovered over mountains, releasing torrents of rain. Water gushed down from the mountains and filled the gorge below. Bodies rose up on the flood water. Dozens of them.

Was this history or prophecy? Thunder was not sure. He followed the line of the flood water to the next image, on Moon's right shoulder blade. It was a magnificent rendering of a dam. *The* dam. The one holding the big river back and the one they had been repairing and rebuilding today. The image showed giants scurrying around the base and top of the dam, carrying boulders like ants carrying eggs.

OK, thought Thunder. Simple enough. The river drowned out the river people and giants tamed the river with the dam.

His eye scanned across Moon's back to her spine. Now here was something interesting. The inker had put the big river exactly down the middle of Moon's back. But it was not a big river at all, not like the one on the first shoulder blade. It was the merest trickle, coursing over the bumps and dips of Moon's vertebrae in a thin blue line. Thunder blinked. He had always thought of the big river as, well, *big*. Moon's back said it was tiny. Thunder thought about the river, about seeing it from the cliff's edge. The inker had it right. The river was small. Thin. Tiny, even. They all called it the big river, but it was big only to the river people.

Thunder examined the rest of the image. Streams branched out from the emaciated river they fed. They snaked away and up, following Moon's ribs to the top of her spine where the mountains stood. The whole thing was a loop. Thunder studied the image. He looked closer. The inker had inked in giants along these streams. Giants holding huge tree trunks, which they dragged along the stream's path.

It this what Moon wanted him to understand?

Thunder tapped Moon's shoulder. She dropped her shirt back over the tattoos and turned around.

You see? she signed.

You're saying we built the streams.

Yes, signed Moon. *We diverted the big river above the dam into dozens of small streams that went around the dam and emptied into the gorge below. Without them, the dam wouldn't have worked. Just holding back the water wouldn't be enough. Without a release of some water below the dam, the river would have disappeared, and the pocket people needed the river. Still do.*

Thunder thought of the streams traversing the land. Some of them were very short. Others were miles and miles long. The giants had created them by sending strands of the big river over the cliffs at various places. Each town had its own waterfall. This was obviously no coincidence or accident, as he had once thought. The giants had put a deliberate plan into action. All to create a world for the pocket people.

So, signed Thunder, *why don't we just make the streams bigger?*

Moon slapped her forehead. Then she slapped Thunder's left temple and his right temple. *Think*, she signed. *The river is going to be too big. It will flood everything: the gorge, the streams, the plateau, and our caves. Everything will be swept away.*

Thunder put his hand up to his temple. It did not seem quite necessary for Moon to convince him of her plan by hitting him.

If you say there's no other way, he signed.

Moon slapped him on the back, this time more a gesture of affection than the exasperation that prompted the temple slaps.

Take the food down to the gorge, signed Moon. *Then come back. We'll leave at first light in the morning.*

Thunder hesitated, but she had a plan and he

didn't, so he reasoned it was best to make hers go as well as possible. He turned toward the cliff and began walking.

He passed other giants, who nodded at him. He nodded back. They were going in the opposite direction, gathering, he supposed, with Moon, getting final instructions before heading up to the mountains.

As he walked he felt small stings around his ankles. He looked down, but could see nothing from so far away in the dark. He kept walking. The stings continued. At first he thought they were bug bites. Then they felt more like rocks. Someone was throwing rocks at him? He stopped and looked around. He was near the dam, in a small clearing where the mud from the repair activities had hardened somewhat in the cool night air. He felt a sting on his heel. He turned around and looked down. Fern stood on the dam. She raised her hand, waving at him.

Thunder put down his burden and went down on one knee.

Hi, he signed.

Man, signed Fern. *You are one slow giant.*

I know. Where did you go?

After I ran from you I was going to go back down to the gorge, but I had to see for myself what was going on up here. I went to see what you were burying.

Thunder's heart thumped audibly. Did Fern still think the giants were all killers? *And...* he signed.

They're all so old, the dead ones, she signed. *We used to live up in the mountains, didn't we? I mean our ancestors.*

It looks that way.

And something happened? They got trapped in a glacier and now the glacier is melting and all those trapped people came tumbling out. It's horrible.

Thunder nodded. *We're going to fix that.*

How?

Never mind right now. I saw Firefly. She was up here.

Firefly was here?.

Yes, signed Thunder. *She came looking for you.*

Fern sighed. *See?* she signed. *I told you she was impulsive. Where is she now? Safe in your cave?*

There's more, signed Thunder. *Her friend Mushroom came up looking for* her.

Fern laughed. *My goodness, I started something didn't I? Soon the whole gorge will be up here living among the giants.*

Fern, pay attention, signed Thunder.

Fern stopped laughing. She looked at Thunder, waiting. Thunder signed nothing.

Yes, signed Fern, still smiling.

I accidentally let Mushroom fall from my pocket.

Fern's smile faded. Her eyes darkened. *And?*

Thunder didn't say anything.

What are you getting at? signed Fern. *Mushroom is ok, isn't he?*

Thunder shook his head. *No, Fern. He's not ok. He died.*

Fern blinked. *Dead? You're telling me Mushroom is dead?*

Yes.

Where's Firefly? She's in your cave, isn't she? Isn't she?

Thunder shook his head. *She's in Dribbleton,* he signed.

Dribbleton? She would never go there. Nothing but fish-eaters there. Something wrong with all of them.

No, signed Thunder, *they're isn't. I'm from Dribbleton, remember?*

Fern ignored the question. *Why is Firefly in Dribbleton?*

That's where they took Mushroom.

Then I need to go to Dribbleton, she said.

Thunder pointed to the top of his pocket. *I'll take you,* he signed. *I'm going that way.*

Fern looked simultaneously sympathetic and disgusted. Thunder wondered how she could do that.

I think I'll go on my own this time, she signed.

Thunder nodded. Of course she wouldn't want to risk the same fate as Mushroom. Fern looked so sad. *They all want to go to the sea,* signed Thunder. *But that's a mistake. You will all drown in the sea.*

The sea? signed Fern. *That makes no sense.*

I know. The giants are going to divert the river. We will save the gorge.

Fern studied him for a long time. Thunder remained kneeling. *Divert the river? Is that even possible?*

Giants have done such things before.

Fern looked doubtful. *If you say so.*

It's not me. It's our wisest elder.

I hope she's wiser than you, signed Fern.

Thunder felt stung. *Maybe I can go down to Dribbleton and get Firefly,* he signed. *Bring her back here to you.*

No, signed Fern. *I don't think you should be carrying any of us for a while. Maybe not ever.*

Thunder nodded. He didn't blame her for thinking that way. She had to go down to Dribbleton herself to find Firefly. Mother and daughter should be together now. *Will you tell Mushroom's parents I'm sorry?* signed Thunder.

Of course.

It was a terrible accident.

I'm sure they know.

Still, signed Thunder. *Tell them.*

OK.

Thunder picked up the net holding the dead

game and walked down the path towards Dribbleton. He walked quickly, leaving Fern far behind. On the gorge floor he dared go only a short distance, not wanting to put any pocket people or their houses in jeopardy. He dropped the dead animals on the ground. Dribbleton probably wouldn't accept the food. He should take it downriver to Craddleton, but Moon said they had to get going, so he couldn't take the time to go to Craddleton. He rose to his full height and surveyed the village before him. Dribbleton had some lanterns on and he saw shapes in the darkness: pocket people moving about. Many of them were on the river, getting the boats provisioned and ready to sail, he supposed. A shadow came toward him. Good. Someone saw he was here. They would find the food. He turned and began walking back up the cliff. He never thought he would feel this way, but he was glad to be leaving the gorge and the pocket people behind. He didn't need any tattoos from them. Moon had the whole history of the giants on her skin. Why add to a saga already depicted so well? He did not feel the itch over his heart anymore. Instead a numbness had settled into him. He was glad Moon had concocted a plan to divert the river. It made his life easier. He would follow Moon to the mountains and with the rest of the giants he would move rocks and dirt with brute force. So simple. A mostly brainless task that used his talents to their full potential.

Near the bottom of the trail, he saw Fern again, descending toward Dribbleton. He stopped and looked down at her. She saw him too. The moon was half way across the sky. Its light illuminated Fern's hands like they were tiny fireflies.

Did you leave the deer? she signed.

Yes.

I heard Firefly screaming. Something about not wanting it.

Thunder sighed. *I was afraid of that, but I did what I could.*

She sounded awful. My baby. I'm afraid to see her now.

She'll be different, signed Thunder. *You have to go down there.*

You look sad in the moonlight, she signed.

I killed a pocket person today, signed Thunder. *If I wasn't sad there would be something terribly wrong with me.*

She wasn't leaving. What did she want here? Her daughter was in Dribbleton. Her life was down there.

Remember the three quarter moon? signed Fern. *How I always said it was better than the full moon. Less light, maybe, but a promise of the future.*

Sure I remember.

Keep that in mind, Thunder. The future is always ahead of us and it can always be brighter.

Not for me, signed Thunder. *I killed one of you. I have no right to be around any of you. From now on, my life will not be in this gorge, or with any pocket person. I'm going to the mountains and I will never come back. I will die there.*

Don't say that, signed Fern.

It's the truth, he signed. *Go be with your daughter now.* He turned from Fern and began walking toward the mountains.

firefly

Firefly fought an urge to run to her mother and embrace her. Since that urge paled in comparison to her other desire, at that moment, to want nothing to do with her mother ever again, it was not a terribly difficult fight.

"Mom," she said. "Nice of you to join us. How's Dad?"

Firefly's mother looked confused. Her mouth moved, like she wanted to say something but could not form the words. She looked past Firefly to Mr. Epiderm.

"She knows all about Thunder," said Mr. Epiderm.

Firefly folded her arms in front of her and tilted her head in a stance which she hoped exuded disgust and the most profound disapproval possible. Her mother's face relaxed and softened. "I'm sorry I never told you," she said.

"Must have slipped your mind, huh?"

"I understand you're angry with me."

"I guess it's easy to confuse the two," said Firefly. "My father died. My father became a giant. Not a lot of difference there. I can see how you had trouble keeping the two stories straight. Only thing is. A dead father couldn't have killed my best friend."

"He's sorry about that," said her mother. "It was a terrible accident. He feels awful."

"Whew," said Firefly. "That makes everything better."

"Why are you like this?" said her mother. "What's going on with you?"

"Besides Mushroom dying? Well, today I find out my father, who I thought was dead since before I was born, is really alive. That's a wee bit of a stunner. Oh, and also, my mother likes to go up on the plateau and spend time with him, which is something she never told me about."

"Today was the first time I went up on the plateau," said her mother. "I've never been there before."

"Is that so? And why should I believe you when you've been lying to me for—how long? Oh yeah. My. Whole. Entire. Life."

"Whatever I did," said her mother, "it was what I thought was best for you."

"And easier for you. You didn't have to tell me

you went with a fish-eater, right? That would have been too embarrassing. Easier to tell me Daddy was dead. Easier to be a liar to your own daughter."

Her mother's face turned a bright red. Firefly did not often see her mother angry. She was usually stern and humorless, also insistent in her wishes, but hardly ever angry. Her mother tightened her hands into fists at her sides. Firefly took a step back and stumbled into Mr. Epiderm, who gently held his hands on her back to steady her.

"I'm giving you the benefit of the doubt," said her mother, "because of what happened to Mushroom. So call me all the names you want, and call your father all the names you want, but when you're done, we need to leave the big river. We need to go up to the plateau and journey to the mountains."

"The mountains?" said Firefly. "Don't be ridiculous."

"It's where we came from," said her mother. "I saw all the people, people like us, who were trapped in the glacier. Firefly, they had been up there for generations. The glacier is melting, which means the mountains will be warmer. It will be a safe place for us. We should all go there."

"Fern," said Mr. Epiderm. "We've all decided our best chance at survival is to sail out to sea."

"No no no," said Firefly's mother, shaking her

head. "I'm not letting my daughter take her chances on the open ocean. None of us are sailors. We would all die."

"The plateau will be flooded," said Mr. Epiderm. "We can't take refuge there."

"Not the plateau," said Firefly's mother. "The mountains. We can live in the mountains. And even if we want to come back here, it is a better place to wait out whatever happens. The giants have a plan. They will save the gorge for us. They're going to change the course of the river."

Firefly looked from her mother, to Mr. Epiderm, then back to her mother again. She could not tell which of them looked more doubtful.

"Did Thunder tell you this?"

"Yes. But it's not only him. All the giants are going to go to the mountains. It will be a big job. If we go we can help them."

Mr. Epiderm looked doubtful. "Fern," he said, "are you sure about this?"

"Yes, yes. I'm sure."

"What a minute," said Firefly. "This doesn't make any sense. What exactly are we supposed to do to help the giants? We can't lift anything. We can't divert any river. I mean, come on."

"It doesn't matter," said her mother. "We are going up there. We are not going to the ocean."

Firefly had never defied her mother before, at

least not in any obvious way, except maybe when she was very young, but she was absolutely convinced going up to the plateau now was a terrible idea. Yes, going to the ocean would be difficult, but at least they would have a chance. No giants would be running around to kill them with their clumsiness. "No," she said.

Her mother looked stunned. "What?"

"I'm not going up to the plateau again and I'm sure not going to the mountain. It doesn't do anyone any good. The giants can do whatever they do, but they'll do it without me."

"You're too young for this, Fern. You are not yet old enough to make your own decisions or to disobey me."

Fern didn't say anything else. She had made up her mind and nothing was going to change it now. She brushed past her mother and went out the door into the streets of Dribbleton. She turned the way the people who had carried Mushroom turned. She went along a narrow street and was soon in the wilderness outside of Dribbleton. The river flowed behind her. The waterfalls cascading down the cliffs were especially loud tonight.

Ahead of her, river people from Dribbleton and Craddleton stood in a circle around Mushroom, who was on the ground at their feet. They held candles in the air. Someone had dug a grave. The dam was on the other side, its mass rising above them, rivaling the sky. Firefly approached the circle. They parted for her, candles moving in the darkness, the flames bending at their wicks like people bowing. Firefly moved slowly. Her feet pressed on the ground, this dirt and vegetation that had sustained her and her people for ages. It was all going to be under water in a couple of days. Maybe sooner. She stopped only a few steps from Mushroom, wrapped in cloth at her feet. She was aware of the cliffs beyond. She remembered being up on the plateau earlier today, how the world went on forever. So different from the gorge, where the walls held everyone in. Why had she never noticed this before? Maybe the Dribbletonians were right. Maybe the river people *were* slaves to the giants. They kept the river people here for their own uses, not caring a whit for their well-being except as it impacted their own.

She felt hands on her shoulders, her arms, her hair. It was foreign contact, being touched by fish-eaters. Firefly welcomed it. Mushroom's parents stood on the other side, facing her. She didn't want to look at them, but could not look away. They acknowledged her with a slight nod. She nodded back.

Two of the Dribbletonians lifted Mushroom and eased him into the grave. Mushroom's mother dropped a clump of dirt onto him. Then his father. Firefly reached down and lifted a handful of dirt herself. She stepped forward and dropped it onto Mushroom.

"Good bye," she said.

"Good bye, Mushroom," said her mother. Firefly turned. Her mother looked back and extended her arm and dropped a handful of dirt onto Mushroom.

The rest of the mourners, each in turn, let slip some dirt from their fingers onto Mushroom. Firefly did not say a word. She turned and stepped away from Mushroom's grave, back toward Dribbleton and the big river.

She listened to the chorus of rough sound, like scratches in the air. This land was to be a lake bottom soon. Everything she had known up to this time would be obliterated. No matter. She was going to the sea. It was sad Mushroom could not join her.

Firefly hurried her pace. Her mother followed. Soon Firefly was at the shore of the big river. Several boats lined the bank. Each of them had a set of oars, ready to propel the craft. The boats also held provisions: blankets, some food, nets. Firefly was a little startled at how small the boats were. Could they survive on the open ocean? It didn't seem possible.

Mr. Epiderm sat in one of the boats. "Please," he said to Fern. "Come in. This is our best hope. We'll stop at Craddleton and get whatever you want from your house. Then we need to get going."

A few boats still dotted the river, but many had already gone with the current toward the sea.

Firefly stepped forward. Mr. Epiderm held out his hand. Firefly took it and stepped over the edge of the boat and onto the deck. It looked like a flimsy craft indeed. Was her mother right? Was this plan a death sentence? No, thought Firefly. It was not. She turned to her mother, who reached out and took Firefly's hand. Firefly pulled it back.

"Please," said Mr. Epiderm. "None of that. Neither of you should be fighting at a time like this."

Firefly's mother reached out again. Firefly slid over to the other side of the boat, which set it rocking. Mr. Epiderm put his hands out to either side, gripping the seat.

"There," said Firefly's mother. "You see? This is ridiculous. You can hardly keep the craft afloat here. What is going to happen in the open ocean?"

"We'll be fine," said Firefly.

"Firefly! Have a little common sense. The people of Paddleton built these boats for easy floating up and down the river, not for ocean voyaging. They are excellent rowboats, but that's all they are."

"I *said* we'll be fine," said Firefly.

Mr. Epiderm struck the rail of the boat sharply with his cane. "Now listen here," he said. "The girl is right. I can't go to the mountains. Neither can a lot of river people. Fern, if you want to go to the mountains, be my guest. But don't hold back those who want to live."

"You would side with my own child against me?" said Fern.

"I merely wish you both to come to some understanding. I need to get going on this boat."

A family of Dribbletonians, a mother, father, and two young children, stepped past Firefly's mother and boarded Mr. Epiderm's craft. He nodded to them. "This family knows what must be done," he said to Fern. "Why don't you see it?"

The boat trembled. Firefly saw the water around her ripple. Everyone looked up. Something was happening on the plateau. Giants were pummeling the earth. Firefly felt a cold shiver goosebump her skin.

The Dribbleton father turned to the cliff. "Infernal beasts," he muttered. He trailed his hand in the shallow water for several seconds. His arm jerked and rose out of the water with a great splashing. He had a wriggling fish in his hand, which he tossed on the deck where it writhed and slapped against the wood. Firefly watched, mesmerized by the futile power of the fish. The man let the fish flop around for a bit, then he picked it up by both hands and brought it to his teeth where he tore the head off and pulled the skin down to expose the flesh beneath it. He ripped off hunks of it and offered a piece to Firefly. Raw fish? She was about to shake her head, then reconsidered. She took the fish, popped it into her mouth, chewed quickly several times and swallowed. It was warm and oily and very pleasant going down. The man's eyebrows went up, and he smiled at her. He offered a piece to Mr. Epiderm, who gladly took it and ate it. The man distributed the rest of the fish to his children and his wife. By the time he had finished only some guts and bones remained of the creature. The man tossed this overboard. Firefly was glad she took the piece. It was her first taste of raw fish and she enjoyed it. "Will you catch another for me?" said Firefly.

"Put your hand in the water," said the man. "When they come up next to your palm, you grab them." He put his hand up and and made a rapid fist. "Like this."

Firefly's mother looked thoroughly disgusted. "Firefly, these are the people you want to be with now?"

The children looked up at her. The parents exchanged glances. "Are we going or aren't we?" said the woman.

Mr. Epiderm turned to Firefly's mother. "Yes, Fern," he said. "We have to make a decision, all of us. Are you with us or are you not?"

Firefly's mother looked at them all. She shuddered.

The boat trembled. Firefly felt the water around her bubble and slap against the boat.

The Dribbleton children in the boat pointed toward the cliff. The mother pulled them closer to her and shouted to the air. "Giants! There are giants coming!"

Firefly saw them. Great dark shapes against the cliff. They moved almost as fast as the group that nearly stepped on her this morning. They swept through Dribbleton, advancing to the river, stepping on Dribbleton houses, scattering dirt and sod every which way.

The Dribbleton father stood up in the boat. "They'll be wanting to kill us," he said. "The giants are coming to kill us all!"

THUNDER

Thunder looked up at the moon as he walked away from Fern. So much left to do, even after a day and night of too much already done and said. He kept walking until he arrived back on the plateau, near the dam. A sharp cold chilled the air. A silvery light cast a cold but agreeable glow on everything, transforming the trees into an icy version of themselves. It was as though the world was a fairy realm, which was something he could understand better than what had happened this last day. When he was a boy Thunder thought of the giants as fairies, mean ones, mostly. All the children of Dribbleton thought the same thing. Giants were bad creatures who only lived to enslave the river people by making them tattoo the giants, clothe the giants, groom the giants, and so on and so on.

When he was becoming a giant himself, all those years ago, Thunder thought it was the worst fate that could befall him, or anyone. Worse than death, even. Now he knew that was absurd. Life was always better than death, no matter if the life you had was not exactly what you had wanted.

When he got up on the plateau, and after he had accustomed himself to his new life, he asked other giants how it happened. How did river people become giants? Many speculated; no one knew. Some believed it had to be a mysterious substance in the water that made certain river people grow. Others thought maybe some plants that grew only in the gorge did something to the growth center of the brain, made it hyperactive. Others contended the abnormal ones were the river people who *didn't* become giants. They were stunted by some mineral in the soil. Those river people who did not ingest the mineral became giants, as was normal. Those that did remained river people, with short life spans and wildly beating hearts. What it amounted to, in this theory, was that river people who did not become giants were essentially poisoned and doomed to a truncated existence.

One of the giants explained to Thunder that all creatures had about the same number of heartbeats: two billion in a lifetime. The bigger you were the slower your heart rate and therefore the longer you lived. To become a giant was to fulfill your destiny as a long-lived creature. Thunder asked why, if it was normal to be this big, did giants have no sense of hearing. This stumped the other giants. Some shrugged, others believed it was a small price to pay for a long and healthy life.

Moon told him the growth spurt caused the bones of giants to get bigger, which meant the bones in the inner ear got bigger too, right along with all the others. The only thing is, the inner ear does not have a lot of room, so the bones got squeezed together and fractured. Without those bones in good working order, normal hearing is impossible.

You see what I mean? signed Thunder then. *If we were normal then why would we lose our sense of hearing? It doesn't make sense.*

Moon had laughed at him. *Why do our teeth crowd together and push themselves out of alignment?* she signed. *Why are our backs so prone to injury? Why do our sinuses clog up and make us miserable? We aren't made perfectly, either as river people or as giants. Life doesn't always make sense. It's just what is.*

Thunder couldn't disagree with her. This past day proved, if proof was needed, how his existence was substantially and spectacularly imperfect and made no sense.

The trees looked like they were standing skeletons, silver bones arranged like a marching army of giants. The image of them stopped Thunder. Was he truly going to go live in the mountains?

A giant approached him. *Are you going with Moon?* he signed.

Of course, signed Thunder. *Isn't everyone?*

No, signed the other giant. *Not everyone. I don't believe we can divert the river. Others agree with me.*

Thunder hesitated. He looked up toward the circle, where he knew giants were gathering, preparing to make the trek to the mountains. *What are you going to do?*

Simple. We're going to pluck some of the pocket people off the river and bring them up here. They can take care of us here. It'll be for their own good. They can't survive in the ocean.

Thunder didn't disagree, although he did not approve of kidnapping the pocket people.

That's not what they want, signed Thunder.

They don't know what they want, signed the other giant.

What an absurd statement, thought Thunder. *They do know what they want,* he signed. *They are very stubborn, you know.*

The giant reached out and punched Thunder lightly on the shoulder. *So are we, my friend. We are at least as stubborn as any of them. After all, we started out as them, didn't we?*

That's what I'm saying. We wouldn't want to be taken against our will. Neither do they.

Their will is going to kill them, signed the giant.

And besides, we're allowed to do what we want. After all, we're bigger than them. He grinned. *Or haven't you noticed?*

Thunder was unsure how to take this giant. Was he serious, or simply deluded? *The caves are going to flood too,* signed Thunder. *We won't have a place to live, much less provide them with a suitable home.*

The giant shook his head. *Sure, the caves will flood, but it'll be temporary. The water will recede and we'll do some cleaning up and it'll be fine.*

Not for them. Not for the gorge.

Now you've got it, signed the other giant. He had an excited expression on his face. *The gorge is done. The river will wipe everything away. But we'll be fine. We'll be ok.*

Thunder studied the giant's face. He appeared perfectly normal, even though he had some ridiculous ideas. He truly believed this was the best thing for the giants *and* the pocket people. Thunder understood the merits of the idea, but making the pocket people do things they did not want to do made him feel uneasy. Sure, the ocean was dangerous, but the pocket people knew the danger. They accepted it. He saw no reason to make them come up here, to a plateau about to be flooded.

There's still time to divert the river, he signed.

The other giant raised his eyebrows. *I don't think so,* he signed. *Look behind you.*

Thunder turned and took a few steps toward the dam. The moon's reflection wavered like flame on the water behind the dam, which had risen alarmingly in the couple of hours since Thunder last saw it. Waves were lapping at the boulders right near the top of the dam. Little more than a couple of feet separated the surface of the plateau from the surface of the water. And the river was still rising. Thunder could see—*any*one could see—the river was rising much too quickly. It would overflow its banks—and the dam—within the hour, maybe in the next few minutes. He turned back to the other giant.

You see, my friend, signed the giant. *Isn't it exactly as I said? The glacier is melting faster than anyone expected.*

Where are the rest of you? signed Thunder.

The giant pointed towards the cliff over his shoulder. *Let's go,* signed Thunder.

They got going. It was dangerous to run in the darkness like this. The moon illuminated the tree tops but did not penetrate very far into the forest. Thunder was essentially stepping blindly. He didn't care. The river people were about to be drowned, and he—yes he, Thunder—was going to save them. Or at least some of them.

Giants joined in a mad rush through the darkness. Trees toppled all around them. The ground shook. They crossed streams swollen to two or three times their normal volume. Since the streams were made of water diverted from the big river near the mountains, it meant a lot more water was coming down from the glacier. The streams could not handle all the overflow. Far too much of it still pushed against the dam.

Thunder and the other giants kept running. He could only imagine what sound they must be making. Giants began sliding down the cliffs. They didn't bother trying to step carefully, or even to protect themselves. They only knew they had to do what they could to save the river people.

Thunder worked up a sweat, even in the chilly night. It sent waves of cold over his skin, but it was not the least bit uncomfortable. It was invigorating, like dousing himself with algae tea. The thought, absurd as it was, made him laugh. The giants threw off great billowing puffs of their breath into the air. Thunder ran close to the cliff. He steered himself over to the edge, kept going, grabbed air, and let himself fly.

He put out his hands, extended his arms to their full length. He was a great cloud floating on the air. No, he was a stupendous thought, made manifest by the mind of the gorge. No, he was the largest bird ever seen. He was all of these things and none of them. He saw a copse of trees on the gorge floor speeding toward him. He tucked himself into a ball and rolled across the little forest, and onto the sand where he lay stretched on the ground like a spent beast, drawing in great volumes of air. Why had be been plodding through his life the past fourteen years? Why had he not done this before? None of the other giants followed his example. They slid and careened down the cliffs. None of them jumped off the cliff. None, perhaps, were quite so foolish.

Thunder rose and looked toward the river. There they were. The river people on their pathetic boats. He stepped toward them. They looked up at him. Some cringed in their boats. Some raised their oars at him. So fierce, they were. He laughed again. Some put their hands on their ears. Some stood and watched him. He stepped into the river, leaned down and put his hand in the water and slid it beneath the surface until his palm was directly under a boat. The oarsman swatted at his arm. Thunder did not let it deter him. He lifted his hand slowly, as gently as he possibly could. The boat rose with his hand. The passengers moved to the center and huddled together. *Good*, he thought. *That's a very good way to protect yourselves.*

He turned. A giant stood behind him. Thunder handed her the boat. She turned and handed it, carefully, slowly, to another giant behind her, and so the rescue went. Giants handing boats full of river people in a line to the cliff and on up to the top.

Thunder waded further into the river. The water lapped at his ankles and then his mid calf. The little rowboats were everywhere. He had only to put his hand in the water and lift. He saw other giants in the river, each one doing as he was doing. Lines of giants snaked from the river back to the cliff. Each line conveyed boat after boat, bearing pocket people, many of whom were hysterical, jumping up and down and waving spasmodically. Others were stoic, accepting the rescue, though not necessarily knowing it even *was* a rescue. The sky was beginning to lighten. Dawn approached. Another day, thought Thunder with a new found joy in his heart.

A lot of the boats were not about to allow this operation to go gracefully. Their passengers rowed madly, with all the strength they could, trying to escape the giants and head downriver to the sea. Thunder never missed his voice as much as he did then. He wanted to tell them they had only one chance now. You stubborn miserable creatures, he thought, let yourselves be rescued. Let us give you life. He lifted up several more boats and handed them off to the line. He and other giants waded further into the river, and chased down the fleeing craft. He put his hand under a boat. All the passengers jumped overboard, into the river. Thunder lifted the empty boat, felt foolish, put it back in the river, and went on to the next boat. The fleeing passengers swam back to the empty boat and climbed inside. This was frustrating. Their stubbornness was going to get them killed. Thunder looked back at the dam. It was still holding, but for how long? That was also where Fern and Firefly were supposed to be. He started going in that direction.

Thunder saw a boat coming from Dribbleton. It looked like it had seven passengers aboard, including the oarsman, who worked hard pulling both paddles through the water. Two of the passengers were children. He got a better look as they rowed closer. His heart skipped a beat. The boat held both Fern and Firefly. He was not about to let this craft get away. He reached down and pinched an oar between his fingers, pulled it away, and dropped it in the river. The oarsman held the other oar in his hands and raised it above his head. Fern stood up in the boat and tried to grab the oar from the man. He pushed back at her. Firefly rose to her feet. Another man in the boat remained seated. Thunder put his hand in the water and moved it under the boat. As he did so, the water level in the river rose by a foot or two as a strong wave came through. The boat rocked and was about to capsize. Thunder stopped it by pressing his palm against its hull. Everyone in the boat turned around and looked in the dam's direction. Their faces were shadowed with fear.

Thunder lifted them out of the water and turned to look at the dam himself.

Several boulders were tumbling down the dam. A massive waterfall had split the dam down the center, dislodging still more boulders, and it was getting bigger by the second. The water coming over the top was flowing very quickly. The mud and branches the giants had wedged between the boulders was all washing away, tumbling down the dam in a thick coursing fall. Thunder looked at the cliff wall. Giants were already running toward it, to escape the river. They knew it was unsafe. They knew if they remained, they would not survive.

firefly

"**D**on't be ridiculous," said Firefly's mother to the Dribbleton man. "The giants don't want to kill any of us."

Firefly looked at her mother. "Mom," she said, "they already did. Don't you get it? They already did."

The Dribbleton man sat back down. His family huddled around him. Firefly watched the children wrap their arms around him like he was the only thing in the world with the power to save them. And maybe he was. The man dropped his oar tips into the water and began rowing away from the bank. Firefly felt the surge of the boat through the water.

"Wait a minute," said Firefly's mother. "You can't take my daughter. Firefly, get out of the boat and come here." Firefly folded her arms and looked away.

Several giants lifted their enormous legs and stepped into the water. Firefly watched them, unbelieving. What on Earth were they going to do in the river? Then she saw. They were lifting the boats right off the surface of the water. She put out her hand, reaching wildly for her mother. Only a few minutes ago she had expected never to want to be near her again. Now she was surprised by her own need for her mother's touch. The Dribbleton man was determined. Firefly's mother jumped from the bank and into the boat, just before it was too late for her to do so.

"Mom!" cried Firefly.

"I'm not letting you go," said her mother. Firefly slid over to the other side of the boat to give her room.

"Welcome aboard," said Mr. Epiderm. His voice was shaky and quiet, like he was more frightened than he wanted to let on. If Mr. Epiderm was afraid, thought Firefly, what hope did any of them have? "We should have left earlier," he said. "But who knew the giants would be coming?"

"You have to believe me," said Firefly's mother. "The giants are not going to hurt us. They want to save us."

"Mom," said Firefly, "they don't care about us. They are so clumsy and stupid. They'll kill us all."

Her mother put an arm around her. "Don't be scared," she said. "They will do what they can to protect us."

Firefly looked up at her mother. Her features were milky, soft and pale in the barely perceptible dawn light beginning to illuminate the sky. Firefly did not understand anything that was happening, but she understood her mother's face, her expression of concern and understanding. Whatever anger she had towards her mother completely disappeared. Firefly was surprised at how quickly it evaporated. Now she could hardly imagine wishing her mother out of her life.

Firefly's mother kissed her cheek and ran her hand over her hair. Firefly moved closer to her, craving the contact.

The Dribbleton man rowed madly. His face was red with the effort. Firefly's mother looked at Mr. Epiderm. "You know him?" she said.

"No," said Mr. Epiderm.

Firefly's mother turned from Mr. Epiderm and addressed the Dribbleton man. "Stop that," she said loudly and slowly, as if the man was hard of hearing and stupid, which Firefly knew he was not. "The rowing is not doing anyone any good. We should remain still in the water so they can take us."

"No!" said the man. "I won't let them take us up

to the plateau. We will die there."

"I've been to the plateau," said Firefly's mother. The man looked at her. "So has my daughter."

Firefly nodded. "We were both there. We're still alive."

Shadows of giant legs drifted across the man's face. The boat floated past a forest of giant legs. The Dribbleton man stopped rowing. He looked left and right at the giants in the river. "What cursed boat have I brought my family to?" he said in a whisper.

"No cursing going on here," said Firefly's mother. "Look around you. The giants are lifting us out of the water, and taking us up to the plateau."

"No," said the man. "No no no. We have to go to the sea." He sat back down and began rowing again, with all his strength. He pulled the oars through the water. The boat was propelled on the current.

Firefly could see the man's efforts were going to be useless. The giants plucked boats from the river all around her. Firefly saw the craft rise in the air, water dripping from the hulls, then pass from giant to giant, away from the big river toward the cliff walls.

Their vessel now came closer to one of the giants. He bent closer. It was her father. His hand came swooping down from the sky. Firefly froze, completely terrified. The Dribbleton mother cringed and cried out. "Oh for river's sake," said Firefly's mother. "Quit your whining."

The giant's hand stopped near one of the oars in the water, pressed it between thumb and forefinger, and removed it from the Dribbleton man's hand so gently Firefly found herself holding her breath. How could something so big be so precise? The man's face turned red. "You see," he shouted. "We are done for. You see?"

He rose up on his feet, grasped the other oar in his hand and began swinging it in the air, hoping, Firefly supposed, to connect with the giant. Firefly's mother stepped across the deck and grabbed the man's hand.

"Fern," said Mr. Epiderm. "I don't think that is the best thing to be doing right now."

"He's endangering us all with his stupid antics," said Firefly's mother. "Help me subdue him."

"Do you forget my circumstances?" said Mr. Epiderm.

"No," said Firefly's mother. "Use your canes on him. Knock some sense into this foolish man."

Firefly felt a rumble behind her. Not the rumble of giants; it felt much bigger than that. She turned around. A high wave advanced toward her. It looked big enough to capsize the boat. "Brace yourselves," said Firefly loudly. "Brace yourselves!"

Firefly could not see how the craft was going to keep from tipping over. The wave rose and pushed the stern of the boat up. Firefly prepared to jump into the river. Before she had to do so, the boat came to a steady stillness and rose above the surface of the river. The giant, her father, had his palm pressed firmly against the hull and kept it from wobbling.

Firefly's mother let the Dribbleton man go. He fell down on the deck of the boat. He pointed in the direction of the dam.

An enormous volume of water plowed over the dam through a gushing wound in the rocks. Boulders peeled off the gash and tumbled down the dam.

Yesterday, when Firefly saw the dam in trouble, it looked completely repairable, and so it was, for a while. Now it looked like it could never be fixed. This breach had an air of finality. The dam was finished and the entire gorge was to be inundated in water.

Firefly's mother came back to Firefly and took her by the shoulders and guided her down to the deck. "Hold on," she said. Firefly nodded. Her mother went to Mr. Epiderm and helped him ease off his seat and slide down to the deck. He was clearly uncomfortable with his legs folded up, but it was necessary for his own safety. The Dribbleton family crouched down in the center of the boat which continued to rise. Firefly prepared to be handed off to another giant. Instead, her father brought his other hand under the boat and, supporting them in his two palms, began walking briskly toward the cliff. Firefly wanted to peek over the edge of the boat, but dared not leave her mother on the deck alone. Instead, she stole peeks at the sky above her. The moon was down. The strengthening sun dimmed the stars. Firefly felt the boat going up again, with her father taking uncertain steps over terrain she did not recognize. He must be taking a giant's trail up the cliff. Before long the boat came to a rest on stable land. Her father stood and looked down at them.

Is everyone ok? he signed.

I'm fine, signed Firefly.

A-OK, signed Firefly's mother.

Where are we? signed Mr. Epiderm.

Firefly's father laughed. *Take a look,* he signed.

Mr. Epiderm dragged himself over to the edge of the boat and looked over. Firefly stood up and looked herself. The Dribbleton family remained huddled on the deck. Firefly saw the dam. It was in an even more dire state of disrepair. The big waterfall down the center had expanded, and three or four newer smaller ones had joined it. The water came down in curtains. She could hardly see the dam at all.

"Oh my," said Firefly's mother. She pointed downriver to the boats still on the water.

"Are they going to be ok?" said Firefly. The river was no longer a well-defined line down the center of the gorge. Instead, it had swollen to at least ten times its usual width. In some places it was already lapping at the cliff walls. And it was still rising.

"I don't know," said her mother.

The water pushed the boats at an incredible speed. From up here they looked like tiny beetles. The river kept widening. The water rolled over houses and water wheels, snapping the wood with loud pops. The water, proceeding in waves and strong surges, scoured out entire villages like they were bits of bark being shaved off a log. Splintered wood floated everywhere. The gorge was filling up with water.

"There are so many," said Firefly. "So many the giants didn't get to."

"They tried," said her mother. "They could not save everyone. No one expected the dam to fail so quickly."

Firefly looked up at her father, who surveyed the scene. He looked like he was in shock. Firefly looked back toward Dribbleton. Mushroom was under all that water. She didn't know exactly what to think about that. She didn't want to imagine him submerged for the rest of time. She didn't want to think of all the river people being pushed to the sea and ending up drowned with the fish.

The Dribbleton family stepped out of the boat and began running away from the cliff edge.

"Where are they going?" said Firefly. "They'll get lost up here. They don't know what to do on the plateau."

"You can't help them," said her mother. "Let them go, Firefly."

Firefly saw other boats along the cliff edge, with giants near them. People stood up on the decks and stepped over the hulls of the boats and put their feet down on the plateau. They were now in a place they had only heard stories about. They could hardly know what to make of their surroundings.

Firefly's mother looked up at her father. *What now?* she signed. *Do you have a place we can go to?*

I don't know, signed her father. *No one expected this.*

Mr. Epiderm cleared his throat. He was turned away from the river, facing the mountains.

"What is it?" said Firefly.

Mr. Epiderm pointed. "I believe we have a new crisis before us," he said.

Firefly looked in the direction of Mr. Epiderm's pointed finger. The sun was not yet completely up.

Still, enough light illuminated the sky for them to see an enormous pure white cloud billow up from the mountains. It looked like a huge mushroom. The cap spread out in slow motion and filled the sky. Bumps and irregular bulbous growths erupted along its stem.

"What is it?" said Firefly. "How can a cloud come up from the mountain?" At the base of the cloud a bright orange light, as though from fire, illuminated the pure white of the vapor, sending spikes of light in a rayed arc towards the top of the cloud. The mountain was on fire.

"I can't be sure," said Mr. Epiderm, "but I don't think that's a cloud at all. What we're seeing is steam coming from the glacier."

Firefly blinked rapidly. "The mountain is a volcano," she said. "Isn't it, Mr. Epiderm?"

Mr. Epiderm nodded. "Yes," he said. "And it has chosen a most inconvenient time to erupt."

THUNDER

The man in the boat signed to Thunder. *Did you know the mountain was a volcano?*

A volcano? Thunder turned around. A pure orange glow, bright as the sun from this distance, illuminated the white cloud rising up from in front of the mountain. Thunder had never suspected the mountain would ever erupt. He turned to the man, who was still looking up at him. Firefly and Fern also had their heads turned up to Thunder. *No*, he signed. *None of us knew.*

So you have no idea what to do about it? signed the man.

We were going to divert the flow of the river, signed Thunder.

Too late for that, signed the man. *The lava is melting the glacier and must have been doing so for some time. It explains the flooding and it's only going to get worse. There will be enough water to fill up the gorge. I think it's also going to flood the plateau.*

Who are you? signed Thunder.

My name is Mr. Epiderm. I am Firefly's tutor. I used to be an inker.

You are crippled? signed Thunder.

An accident during inking. It was a long time ago. What about the flooding?

The canals no longer held water between their banks. Instead, the overflow from upstream was spreading across the plateau. Thunder saw the water coming across and sliding against the tree trunks. They were on a slight rise here at the edge of the cliff, so they were still on high ground for now, but that wasn't going to last. He stood, bewildered by these new developments. He thought all he had to do was bring the people in the boats up here and all would be fine. It was not turning out that way at all.

I can take you to my cave, signed Thunder.

Fern signed up to him. *That won't do any good. It's not high enough.*

She was right. Flood water was already pouring out of the forest. It began lapping at Thunder's feet. He looked at it dumbly. The forest was releasing water? Rivulets pushed past him towards the cliff edge, widening to sheets of water before slipping out of sight and adding their volume to the immense quantities already in the gorge.

We have to go to the mountain, signed Fern. *It's our*

only hope.

Thunder tried hard to make himself see the wisdom in this. It wasn't happening for him. Why would they go toward the source of the problem? *No,* he signed. *That's backwards thinking.*

No, it's not, signed Fern. *It's sideways thinking.*

A group of giants approached Thunder. They still held their boats in their hands.

Where are you going? he signed.

They didn't answer. Instead, they shrugged their shoulders, as if to say their hands were occupied and could not communicate with him. Thunder reached out to them as they went by. They shook off his hand and kept walking. They were going toward the circle of stones. Thunder decided to follow them. He bent down and reached to pick up the boat. Fern, Firefly, and Mr. Epiderm all huddled together in the middle of the boat. He thought about lifting them up to his shirt so they could ride in his pocket, but he remembered the accident with Mushroom and did not want to commit a similar episode. Instead, he lifted the boat off the ground and held it in his hand. Holding them like this would be fine. He would be careful. They could grab onto the rim of the boat for stability.

Thunder began walking toward the circle of stones. Other giants followed. As he walked, Thunder studied the steam and the glow in the distance.

The gorge was finished. Even if the dam could be rebuilt now, all the villages of the river people were completely destroyed. They would have to rebuild from scratch.

Of course the giants could help, but even with their building materials and their food, the people of the gorge might no longer have the will to return. It might be better for them to live up here on the plateau with the giants. Except there wasn't going to be a plateau. At least, not the way it had been up to now.

The throngs of giants grew thicker as Thunder neared the circle. He slogged through the water, which was ankle deep now. He was beginning to lose his bearings in this new waterscape. The trees were still there. The landmarks he had always counted on—the gorge, the dam, the cliff edges, and the caves—were all obliterated, or in the process of disappearing. This was worse than when he transitioned from a pocket person to a giant. At least then he knew there was something else to go to, however alien. Now he wasn't sure they had any options.

He turned a corner, following the group of giants. He came to a group of dozens of giants, each of them holding aloft a row boat built by the carpenters of Paddleton. Each craft held at least one pocket person, most with closer to five or six. The giants filled the spaces between the rocks in the circle. Moon stood on the slight rise just to the east of the rocks. The cloud of steam in the distance appeared to be growing out of the top of her head. Thunder took a place behind the giants, facing Moon.

We have been through this before, she signed. *The mountain has erupted in the past. Its lava came down here and made the caves we live in. It spread over this land and created the plateau. Later the river came through and carved out the gorge, but before that was the lava.*

The giants watched her sign with complete attention. Moon was widely considered to be the wisest of any giant. She was the oldest and had the most tattoos. Many giants believed Moon had the entire history of their world tattooed on her skin. All anyone—giant or pocket—had to do to read the past was to look at Moon's tattoos.

A giant toward the front signed something to Moon.

I have been asked a question, signed Moon. *Crow wants to know if we should still try to divert the river.* Other giants nodded and held up their hands in a gesture that communicated assent. They all wanted to know what to do next.

No, signed Moon. *When the river was fed by a slowly melting glacier, we had a chance to dig new canals. But now, with the glacier rapidly dissolving, the river is going to be much too big to re-channel. What we must do is—*

Moon never finished her sentence. All the pocket people in the boats became very agitated. The boats rocked and jiggled in giant hands. The pocket people pointed to the mountain. Thunder looked in that direction. The steam was still there, as was the orange glow, but now something new: gray ash colored the steam cloud. It pushed its way through and up the center of the steam, twice as tall as the white billowing cloud. The wind at the higher elevations pushed against the pillar of ash and began to sweep it across the sky. Thunder also saw great chunks of rock thrown up and lofted aside from the mountain like they were nothing more than pine cones blown in wind.

The ground quaked against the soles of Thunder's feet. The pocket people in the boats held their hands to their ears. Incredibly loud explosions must be accompanying the eruptions. Thunder's instinct was to put Fern, Firefly, and the man into his pocket and run. But where would he run to?

Moon held up her hands again. The giants looked toward her. *Everything now depends on us,* she signed. *We must save everything.*

I already know that, thought Thunder. The question is, how? Some of the giants weren't waiting to find out. They had already turned from the mountain and were heading along the cliff edge toward the sea. Thunder understood their thinking. Anyone would want to get away from the mountain now, but the sea could not offer them any real hope of salvation. They had no knowledge of the sea, no way to live on it. None of the giants were boat builders.

Wait, signed Moon. *Don't go! We need you.*

The giants who were leaving did not turn around. Thunder wanted to stand in front of them, or grab them by the shoulders. Anything to keep them from marching to their doom.

The plateau had become the top of an expansive waterfall. All around him the pooled water slipped over the cliff and tumbled down to the rapidly filling gorge.

Moon pointed to the sky. *Look up,* she said.

Thunder and the few remaining giants in the circle all lifted their heads. Great flocks of crows flew over them. They were going in the direction of the mountain, toward the steam and the lava.

The crows have wisdom beyond ours, signed Moon. *We should follow the crows.*

Thunder had to think about Moon's words. This was her advice, her sage counsel to them? Follow the crows? Thunder tapped the giant in front of him on the shoulder. He turned. Thunder handed him the boat holding Fern, Firefly, and the crippled man, Mr. Epiderm. The other giant took it. Thunder raised his hands so Moon could see him.

Crows are carrion eaters, signed Thunder. *They will not lead us to life.*

Not only carrion, signed Moon. *They eat living food. Nuts, seeds, fruit.*

So you are saying we will find food by following them?

Food and more. Crows are the ultimate survivors. They will always find a way to live.

They know how to survive as crows, signed Thunder, *but none of us are crows. We are pocket people and giants. We need things other than what crows need.*

Moon looked annoyed with him. *The pocket people used to live in the mountains.*

Yes, signed Thunder. *And they died there. Do we want to go there so we can die?*

The pocket people are our responsibility. The best we can do for them now is take them to the mountain.

The mountain that is erupting and spewing hot ash and throwing up rocks, signed Thunder.

Other giants raised their hands in fists. They signed their distrust of following the crows. Crows made nests in the hair of the giants. They were followers, not leaders. Anyone could see that.

My friends, signed Moon. *You have known me all your lives. You know I owe my life to the pocket people, and would do nothing to harm them or bring them to ruin. Why do you not accept my proposal as right and necessary?*

Glowing embers rained down from the sky in bright streaks. Most of them fell into the water and fizzled out in a burst of smoke and steam. Others fell on trees, igniting fires that quickly spread to other trees. Thunder put one hand up over his head to shield himself from the hot missiles. He grabbed the boat with his other hand and put it up to his shirt pocket. He could spare no more time for talking or cradling this stupid rowboat. He had to do something to protect these pocket people. They hesitated in the boat. Thunder rocked it gently so they would get the message. Eventually they each climbed out of the boat and slid into his pocket. Thunder tossed the boat aside. It fell into the water and quickly slipped over the edge of the cliff and disappeared. The water from the overflowing streams was well over his ankles now, and very cold. As much as he hated to admit it, Moon was probably right. They had no choice anymore except to wade through the flood toward the mountain, if only to get to higher ground.

The crows were thick and black against the sky. Fires raged around him. Thunder took large steps away from the plateau. Other giants followed him. Fern and Firefly put their hands up to the top seam of his pocket and poked their heads over the edge to look around. Mr. Epiderm remained down at the bottom. Thunder thought how inconvenient it was to be transporting a crippled man. He would be no use at all to anyone. Everyone who was going to trek to the mountain needed to be in good shape.

Most of the other giants followed Thunder's example. They coaxed the passengers out of the boats and into their pockets. Smoke was beginning to get thicker. It obscured the view like a thick fog. Thunder turned toward the mountain, which he supposed he had to now call a volcano. He felt a scratching at his chest and looked down. Fern signed up to him. *We need to get going.*

Thunder bit his lip. He put up his hands. *I know,* he signed.

My friend is not in the best of shape. The sooner we get going, the better.

You want to go up to the volcano? signed Thunder.

What choice do you have? What choice do any of us have?

Now Firefly raised herself up on the seam of Thunder's pocket and supported herself on her armpits. She put out her hands. *Mom's right,* she signed. *Mr. Epiderm needs to get up to higher ground where he can be more comfortable. He got hurt inking you giants. The least you can do is find him a decent place to live.*

Thunder was annoyed. Why were Fern and Firefly telling him what to do? Even he could see they had only one option now. He stepped forward, slogging through the water. The soles of his feet scraped against trees way down beneath the surface. The water had some force behind it. He stepped to the side, trying to get away from the full onslaught. The weight and current, the sheer immense volume of it, was threatening to push him over, and such a thing must not happen. The passengers in his pocket would then surely die, and he himself might not be able to get up.

Fern kicked at his chest vigorously. Thunder looked down at her. Not now, he thought, I can't talk to you now.

Do you see? signed Fern. *Do you see what's in front of you?*

Thunder looked up. What had previously been a discoloration in the cloud was now much more. A bright red and orange river snaked down the mountain, splitting it and revealing its hot interior in an incandescent fissure. The mountain was about to fracture in two. Thunder watched, in fear and awe, as the rock on either side of the gash crumbled and fell away, and great spouts of hot lava pushed the mountain aside, like it was a jacket the lava needed to discard. The lava looked inexhaustible, and all of it, every last red globule, was moving rapidly down the slope of the ground directly towards Thunder.

firefly

"Mom," said Firefly. "Do you see that?"

"What's going on up there?" said Mr. Epiderm, stuck at the bottom of the pocket and huddled over to one side. Firefly tried hard not to step on him.

"The mountain is disintegrating," she said.

"He has to get to higher ground," said Mr. Epiderm. "Tell him he has to get out of the way of the lava."

"That's what I've been doing," said Firefly's mother. "I think he's getting the idea."

"Good," said Mr. Epiderm.

"The only thing is," said Firefly's mother, "there's fire everywhere. And smoke."

"He needs to get upwind, and on higher ground. Tell him."

Firefly looked up at her father as her mother signed the words. He stared out blankly, as though he did not know where to go or what to do. Seeing him so powerless made Firefly feel more scared than ever. If the giants, who *lived* up here, didn't know where to go, what chance did any of the river people have? Her mother must have gotten through to him. He finally turned into the wind and began walking. He put his hand up to his face, to cover his eyes and mouth. Firefly slipped down to the bottom of the pocket. She crouched right beside Mr. Epiderm. It was darker in the pocket, but enough dim light filtered in through the needle holes along the seams for Firefly to see he was in real pain. Having his legs folded up like this could not be very comfortable at all.

"Is there anything I can do?" said Firefly.

Mr. Epiderm shook his head. "It's this pocket," he said. "I'm no longer made for this mode of travel. If I ever was."

Firefly's mother dropped down from the top of the pocket. "I never thought I'd see a day like this," she said.

"None of us did," said Mr. Epiderm.

"What are we going to do?" said Firefly.

"There's nothing we can do," said Mr. Epiderm. "Our lives are in their hands, the giants." He pointed to Thunder's chest, rising and falling with his inhales on the other side of the shirt. "Actually, in one giant's hands. *His.*"

"That's not such a safe place to be," said Firefly.

"She's right," said her mother. "He can be clumsy. Fatally so."

"And even if he gets us to high ground," said Firefly, "what then?"

"If he can get us away from the water, the ash, the lava, and the smoke, we wait it out. This will all clear away eventually."

Her father settled into a steady trot. They bounced up and down in a regular pattern. The three of them jostled against each other. Firefly tried to push away from Mr. Epiderm, who was having difficulty trying to keep from crowding Firefly's mother. It was almost impossible for everyone to keep their distance from one another and Firefly began to feel cramped and uncomfortable.

The pocket convulsed and a noise like a series of explosions ripped the air.

"What was that?" said Firefly.

"I expect he's coughing," said Mr. Epiderm. "The smoke must be getting to him."

"This is awful," said Firefly's mother.

Mr. Epiderm nodded.

"I'm going to go up and take a look around," said Firefly.

"No," said her mother. "Stay here. It's not safe for you up there."

"It's not safe anywhere," said Firefly.

Mr. Epiderm gave a small laugh. "She's right, Fern," he said.

"Very well," said her mother. It sounded like she was about to start crying. Firefly hesitated. Maybe she shouldn't go up? But she couldn't stay here. It was getting too difficult. She was trying not to be scared, but with all the adults around her expressing their own fears in one way or another, it was not exactly the best circumstances in which to keep up her own courage.

Firefly pushed against the bottom seam of the pocket and reached up to the top edge. She pulled herself higher so her head poked out of the pocket. Billows of smoke and ash filled the air. Firefly closed her eyelids almost completely, so she had only tiny slits to look through. It was dark, but she did see some lightening in the distance, and it looked like her father was heading in that direction. Could he breathe up there? Firefly could not see well enough to be able to tell. More convulsions and explosions came. This could not be good for his lungs.

Firefly dropped back down to the bottom of the pocket. "Well?" said her mother.

"I could hardly see a thing."

"There, you see. Didn't I tell you that?"

"Yes Mom, except I could tell we were getting

to a clearing. Or something."

They remained silent for a while, probably about fifteen minutes. The smoke got into their eyes and lungs and Mr. Epiderm coughed convulsively several times. Firefly's throat felt raw and dry. Her mother stroked her hair and murmured soft assurances to her.

Her father slowed down. Firefly felt enormously grateful. Her father's chest still expanded and contracted rapidly as they finally came to a stop. He was still coughing, but it did not sound too awful. Mr. Epiderm was a little better too. The pocket began tilting. It was the oddest sensation, as if the world was toppling over.

"Hang on," said Firefly's mother.

Firefly grabbed for her. Mr. Epiderm gritted his teeth and tried to hold very still. The pocket ended up horizontal. Her father's breaths did not stop, but they began slowing down. He coughed several times. The pocket bounced and rippled. Firefly and her mother crawled along the front wall of the pocket, which was now the floor, all the way to the edge. Firefly looked over the brim of the pocket. She saw grass and wildflowers a few feet below her. She could jump down easily.

"It's not too far down," said her mother to Mr. Epiderm.

Firefly turned around and let her legs dangle

over the brim, then let go. She fell to the ground and rolled along the grass. Her father's chest was a second sky above her. She got on her feet and ran out from under him. He was on all fours, with his head touching the ground and his shirt very close to the grass. He continued coughing. The sound of it was shocking, like a storm rattling the world.

"Come on," she yelled to her mother, who nodded at her, turned around, and went back into the pocket to retrieve Mr. Epiderm. A couple of seconds later they stuck their heads out from the top of the pocket. Firefly's mother let herself tumble to the ground. She rose and reached for Mr. Epiderm, who put out his hand. Firefly ran over and took his other hand. They eased Mr. Epiderm out of the pocket until he dropped to the ground. Firefly's father rolled away from them and fell on his back, still coughing and wheezing.

Mr. Epiderm, with Firefly and her mother's help, unfolded his legs and stretched out on the grass himself. He looked relieved, which Firefly liked to see. When she was sure Mr. Epiderm was as comfortable as possible, she looked up from the ground and surveyed her location. Crows were everywhere: on the grass, in the trees, strutting on rocks. And more kept coming, streaming in from the fire and smoke. Firefly had never seen so many crows. They filled the air with their calls.

She turned her attention from the crows to try to see exactly where she was. Her father had brought them to a high grassy hill. Below them a large talus field spread down to a thicket of trees. The mountain, or what was left of it, smoldered in the distance, still bubbling up lava in a steady flow. Smoke and steam rose from the surface, was caught by the wind, and dispersed away from them. Firefly estimated the mountain, or what was left of it, was at least five miles away, maybe more. The glacier was mostly melted. Large chunks of it, melting rapidly to billowing steam, rode down the river of lava towards the gorge where Firefly used to live. The lava was hardening as it went, with more lava following it, hardening over top of it, only to be overtaken by more lava following and more layers. They could never return to the gorge.

They were high enough here to see the ocean. A line of water still snaked from the other end of the gorge to the sea, but it was being overtaken by the newly forming rock. Firefly wished she could see if boats still floated in the gorge, but she was too far away to tell.

Firefly's father rolled over on his side and cleared his throat. He pushed himself to a seating position. Other giants came up the hill. They carried river people in their pockets. The giants stopped at the hill and unloaded their passengers, who mostly stood on the grass, bewildered and uncertain what to do. Yes, they were safe for now, but they had no food, no shelter, and no method of locomotion, except by way of the giants. And even if they were able to get around, they had no place to go to. Firefly's father looked as dazed as the newly arrived river people. He rose to his feet, still coughing, and went down the hill. Firefly hoped it was to get provisions for them.

Firefly's mother went to the new arrivals and greeted them as lost relatives, which, Firefly supposed, they were, in a way. The giants who brought them turned around and went down the side of the hill.

Firefly saw two young children, a boy and a girl, had joined them. They appeared to be alone. She ran to them and hugged them. "It's going to be all right," she said. They were crying, and Firefly didn't believe her own words.

"What are your names?" she said.

Between sobs the girl said her name was Cliff and her brother's name was Bridge.

"Where are your parents?" she said.

"We don't know," said Cliff.

"What town are you from?"

"We live on the river."

"I know," said Firefly gently, "but where on the river?"

Cliff and Bridge both looked at her dumbly. Firefly bit her tongue. Her mother put her hand on her shoulder.

"We're going to have to build some shelter," she said to Firefly.

"How?" said Firefly. "There's nothing here."

A group of children came over to Firefly. Cliff and Bridge melted into the group. They all went up the hill a short distance and stood looking into the forest. Firefly hoped the two siblings would be ok with the rest of the kids.

Some of the the giants returned up the hill. They carried wood in various sizes, from kindling for fires to thicker logs for making lean-tos. One of the giants still had a rowboat. She placed it on the ground. Water sloshed from it. Firefly had not even thought about where they were going to get water, and here was a giant doing their thinking for them and providing a water supply. Giants tore off their pockets and the cuffs of their shirts and trousers and put them down on the grass.

For tents, they signed.

Firefly's mother signed back at them. *Thank you.*

The giants nodded. *We'll get more wood. And we'll bring you food.* The giants turned around and plunged back into the woods. Firefly estimated the population of the hill at about seventy or eighty river people. Some stood silently watching the volcano. Others huddled on the ground, unable to move from the shock and fright. Most of them, though, began building fires and constructing tents out of the material the giants had left them. Her mother was busy organizing a group to do the cooking. Firefly found two good sturdy sticks in the pile of wood and brought them over to Mr. Epiderm, who had managed to sit up and looked better, but was still obviously in some pain. "I got these for you," said Firefly.

Mr. Epiderm took the sticks. "Thank you so much, Firefly," he said. "These will help me get around," he said.

Firefly nodded and smiled.

"Are the giants going to bring us food?"

"Yes," said Firefly.

"That's good," said Mr. Epiderm. "We might be here for a while." He looked past Firefly to the gorge in the distance. Smoke rose in the air. The hardening lava that now filled the gorge where they had all once lived was clearly visible as a long gash cutting through the landscape. "There were so many of us," whispered Mr. Epiderm. "Is this all that is left?"

Firefly could not get used to hearing doubt and fear in Mr. Epiderm's voice. He had always been the one who saw the possibility in everything. He was always talking about sideways thinking, always telling her nothing was as bad as it seemed.

"Maybe the boats got to the sea," said Firefly. "You never know. They might have saved themselves, Mr. Epiderm. Maybe the river people will become the ocean people."

Mr. Epiderm did not laugh or even acknowledge Firefly's remark. It was as though all the life had been drained from him. "We can't be ocean people," he said.

"But Mr. Epiderm, you wanted to go to the ocean. You said it was our best hope."

"That's what I thought," he said, "but there are too few of us now, Firefly. I'm afraid we may be the last generation of our kind."

"Mr. Epiderm, you can't think that way. There's always hope. We can change."

Mr. Epiderm nodded. "Yes," he said. "We can change, but we have nothing to offer the giants anymore. We can do nothing for them here with our meager supplies and even smaller numbers. They will not want to do for us much longer. The bond between the giants and the river people will dissolve. It may already have dissolved."

Firefly was stunned. Did Mr. Epiderm truly believe these things? It didn't make any sense. The giants *were* them, after all. Every giant began as a river person. They would not abandon them now, would they? Not when the river people needed their help more than ever.

"We'll live without them if we have to," said Firefly. She indicated all the activity around them with a wave of her hand. People had already put up tents and started a couple of fires. In general, a semblance of civilization was growing around them. "You see, Mr. Epiderm. The river people can do for ourselves if we have to." She spread her hands in the sign language way of indicating everything would be fine, but as she did so, she felt a sharp pain in her fingers.

Mr. Epiderm did not notice the grimace on her face. "Yes, yes, I see," he said.

Firefly's heart fluttered. Why did her fingers hurt? She spread them out again. A sharp jolt of pain stabbed at her joints. This time Mr. Epiderm did notice. "What's wrong?" he asked. "Did you injure yourself?"

Firefly tried to ignore the pain. "I know," she said, not wanting to let go of their conversation, "we'll all *become* giants. That way we can take care of ourselves better than anything."

Mr. Epiderm allowed a small smile to curl his lips, but he was distracted. "Let me feel your hand, Firefly," he said.

"It's nothing," she said.

"Please, Firefly. Indulge me."

Firefly reluctantly put her hand out. Mr. Epiderm took it gently in his own hand and applied very light pressure to the joints of her fingers. "Does that hurt?" Firefly nodded. "For how long?"

"I only just noticed," she said.

Mr. Epiderm's face darkened.

"What is it?" said Firefly. "Is something wrong?"

"Your bones are getting bigger, Firefly," he said.

"Bigger?"

"Yes."

"What does that mean?"

"It can mean only one thing," said Mr. Epiderm. "I'm afraid you are becoming giant." He tried to make his lips smile, but it was an obvious strain. "Congratulations," he said.

Congratulations? How could he say such a thing? This was nothing to be happy about. Firefly never wanted to be a giant. Giants were too big. They were lonely. They were clumsy. They couldn't take care of themselves. They hurt people. They *killed* people. Oh, this was the worst thing that could happen to anyone. Firefly would never have a child of her own. She would never fall in love. Giants did not love. They couldn't love.

"No," said Firefly. "Mr. Epiderm, it can't be. I don't want to be a giant."

"The indications are unmistakable," said Mr. Epiderm. "Being a giant is your best chance at survival anyway, especially now. You should be happy."

Happy. Firefly tried to see it in that light but could not. "How did this happen?" she said.

"It's a mystery," said Mr. Epiderm. "I have tired to figure it out myself, but never have."

"How long?" she asked.

"You mean when will you start growing?"

"Yes."

"I think you already are. That's the pain you're feeling. I expect you'll start noticing a difference in a few days."

A few days? That wasn't enough time to get used to such a thing. "It's going to hurt, isn't it?"

"A little. But that goes away once your body gets used to it."

A thought struck her. "Mr. Epiderm," she said. "I'm going to be deaf!"

Mr Epiderm nodded. "Yes," he said softly. "I'm afraid that's true, Firefly."

Cliff came to Firefly and tugged on her shirt. Firefly hardly noticed. She stared at the crows around her and tried to understand what was going to happen to her. Mr. Epiderm touched her hand. He pointed to the little girl. "It looks like you have a friend," said Mr. Epiderm. "And it looks like she needs something from you."

Firefly looked down at Cliff. "Yes," she said, "what is it, sweetheart?"

Cliff cupped her hand beside her mouth. Firefly bent down to listen. Cliff put her mouth close to Firefly's ear. "We found a dead giant," she whispered.

THUNDER

Once Thunder released his passengers, he trudged wearily through the forest. His lungs and throat felt raw, like he didn't want to draw air over them ever again. It was too painful. He could use some water. Some nice algae tea would be even better, but there was no possibility of that now. He could see it as well as anyone. The mountain had split open and destroyed everything they knew in the gorge and on the plateau.

Here, in the forest around the hill, an abundance of game thrived. Deer fled the conflagration at the mountain and ran right into the giants, Thunder included, who were arrayed in a line to catch them.

Moon walked up to him. *How are you?* she signed.

Fine, signed Thunder.

Are you ok with this duty?

Thunder shrugged. *We have to do what we have to do.*

You could go gather material for making blankets, signed Moon. *There are plenty of giants here to catch game. The pocket people will need other things for their survival.*

This is all temporary, isn't it? signed Thunder.

What do you mean?

They can't live on that hill forever. We can't keep bringing them water in rowboats.

Moon shrugged. *There is no limit to what any of us, giant or pocket, can do if we have to.*

My family is on that hill, signed Thunder.

And many families are simply gone now. This tragedy is much bigger than you, Thunder.

Thunder nodded. *Do you have any grand plan now for our future? What should we be doing to save ourselves?*

There are several ideas. Some think we should each take a few pocket people and strike out on our own, each going in separate directions. A diaspora that would probably ensure survival for many. It might be better than all of us trying to find one place where we can all live. You could take your daughter and her mother if you wanted to.

Are you serious? said Thunder.

Of course.

Has anyone asked the pocket people about this? They wouldn't want to split up what is left of them.

Moon shook her head. *Thunder,* she signed, *you*

must stop believing the pocket people know what's good for them. They do not.

You can't make me believe that.

You must believe it.

Thunder no longer wanted to argue the point with her. *If we all go our separate ways*, he signed, *we would be conceding that our society was finished.*

In a way, signed Moon. *But we have been separated before. You yourself have not always been so interested in sticking with family.*

What do you mean?

Remember, signed Moon, *when we first met.*

Sure, signed Thunder. *I was just a boy.*

Moon nodded. *No more than twelve or thirteen, I think. You climbed up the vines to see what was on the plateau.*

Thunder shrugged. *I was curious.*

Yes, curious. But none of your people in Dribbleton had ever been curious. You defied your own family by climbing up to the plateau.

I suppose so, signed Thunder. *But what of it? I was a rebellious boy. The vines were there. They practically begged to be climbed.*

Not every boy or girl in the gorge climbed those vines. In fact, very few have.

Like I said. I wanted some adventure.

Which is part of what I liked about you. I found you wandering around in the woods.

I remember, said Thunder.

You knew sign language. No one from Dribbleton knew sign language.

Thunder shrugged. *I learned it by watching the inkers over in Craddleton. They were always signing to the giants as they did their tattoos.*

There, you see? You went to Craddleton, you came up to the plateau. You never had the commitment to family and home that so many of the pocket people have. You told me then, the first time you came up to the plateau, you wanted to be giant one day.

No! signed Thunder.

Oh yes, signed Moon.

It must have been something a kid says. Not meaning it.

Moon raised her eyebrows. *Perhaps. And yet, here you are. A giant.*

No one has control over that, signed Thunder.

Moon shook her head vigorously. *Stop insisting you are powerless,* she signed. *It does you no good.*

A flash of white caught their attention. They both looked down and saw a deer, tail flipped up, jumping through the woods. Moon lifted a foot and tried to step on the creature. It bounded to the side and Moon's foot landed on a patch of moss. This was harder to do without nets.

Thunder saw where the deer was going. It was heading for a denser grouping of trees, trying to get to a place where it would be camouflaged. Thunder saw its route laid out on the forest floor like it was a path etched by lava. The deer would jump over this bush here, bound to that tiny clearing, then around the adjacent snag, and through a patch of ferns to a thicker group of trees. All Thunder had to do was put a hand down near the ferns at the right moment and the deer would leap into it and he could close his fist and kill it.

He did not do so. Instead, he watched the animal do exactly as he predicted. Watched and understood the beauty of its machinations, how it used the woods to preserve its own life. In a few seconds it was gone. Perhaps to live for years and years, perhaps to be caught by another giant, up the line. Thunder hoped it would be the former.

Moon looked at him. *You could have caught it,* she signed. *I saw you calculating its path. What happened?*

I decided the pocket people should capture their own food, he signed.

Ah, signed Moon. *They need to learn self sufficiency, is that it?*

Yes. Something like that.

Such a noble sentiment.

Thank you, signed Thunder.

I'm sure the pocket people will feel noble as they starve to death.

Thunder turned from her, not wanting to see anymore of her words. He walked back towards the hill, where Fern, Firefly, and the remaining pocket people were waiting for giants like him to save their lives. But the giants can't save anyone, thought Thunder. The giants could not keep back the river, the mountain, or the lava. The pocket people could learn to look after themselves. They once lived on the mountain. Those bodies on the river proved that. If they could live on the mountain, they could live anywhere.

He glanced back over his shoulder, to see if Moon was following him. She was not. Relieved, Thunder slowed his pace and looked for some water to soothe his throat. He saw a small lake in the middle distance and walked toward it. He carefully knelt down at the edge and dipped his hand into the water and brought some up to his mouth. It felt cool and healing going down his throat. He scooped up several more handfuls and drank until he was no longer thirsty. He kept bringing up handfuls of water, kept swallowing it all down until his stomach felt stretched and full. He felt fish wriggling in the water. He carefully spread his fingers so they would fall through the spaces and back into the lake.

It would not be so bad here for the pocket people. They could make a life in these hills. They could.

And what of me? he thought. Could I live here? Do I want to? He looked back at the mountain and the gorge. Giants still toiled there, putting out the fires. Smoke still colored the sky, but it was dissipating. The lava still churned out of the mountain, which now looked like a small bump on the landscape.

Thunder noticed flashes of motion at his feet. He looked down, expecting to see deer. Instead, a tight pack of several pocket people came into view. They had left the hill and were traveling in the direction of the gorge. Thunder put his foot down in front of them. They stopped and looked up.

Ho there, signed Thunder. *Where are you off to?*

The six pocket people said something to one another, then one of them signed up to him. *We're going back home.*

Thunder shook his head. *There is no home to go back to. It's still dangerous there, with the lava still flowing.*

It'll stop. We don't like it here. We want to go back home.

They drew closer together, as though the comfort of physical contact would help them survive. Maybe Moon was right, the pocket people did not have sense enough to survive on their own. They moved to go around Thunder's foot. Thunder planted his other foot next to the first, again blocking their way.

They all stopped and looked up at him again.

We don't want to be here, one of them signed. *There's a dead giant on the hill.*

Dead giant? *What do you mean?* signed Thunder.

She's in the woods higher up the hill. Looks like she's been dead for a while.

A while? What were these pocket people talking about? *Even if that's true,* signed Thunder. *You can't go back home. None of us can.*

We'll manage, signed the pocket person. *Now will you please remove yourself so we can go?*

Thunder wanted to scoop them up and carry them back to the hill, but what good would that do? They would still want to leave, and he could not watch them every minute of the day. If they wanted to go back to the gorge, they would see it was foolish to try to live there. Then they would return.

Do you have food? signed Thunder. *Water?*

The pocket person looked blankly at him, as though thinking about such necessities was beyond him. *We just want to go,* he signed. *Please let us proceed.*

Thunder stepped away from the group. They hurried on without acknowledging him. Thunder supposed they were propelled by fear. Or the energy of ignorance. He was confident they would be back. He looked up toward the hill. A great flock of crows hovered over it.

Thunder wanted to hear the crows. He knew they must be calling. He had memories of those calls. He watched the crows for a few more minutes. Moon had said the crows would lead them to life. Maybe that was true. And maybe it wasn't.

He drew in a breath, placed a foot forward, and continued up the hill.

firefly

Firefly stood up.

"What is it?" said Mr. Epiderm. "You look pale."

Firefly looked at Cliff. "Are you sure?" she said. Cliff nodded. Firefly put out her hand. Cliff grasped it. "I have to go," she said to Mr. Epiderm. "Show me where," she said to Cliff.

Cliff began running to the summit of the hill. Firefly followed her. They got to a grouping of trees and kept going into the forest. The woods here were familiar, like the woods on the plateau, but with some differences. Fewer ferns populated the forest floor here, and some of the trees were thinner, not as lush. Firefly supposed the weather must be harsher. Cliff moved with a determined pace. She pulled on Firefly's arms. "Slow down," said Firefly. "If it really is a dead giant, it's not going anywhere."

The ground leveled off a bit. They approached

the top of the hill. Soon Firefly saw a clearing ahead. Cliff released Firefly's arms and ran at full speed into the clearing. Firefly stepped out of the woods and onto a patch of grass. Crows flocked everywhere. They swirled over the meadow in a thick cloud. In the center of the meadow a giant, covered in tattoos, lay on her belly. Some children ran around the giant, laughing and screaming, as though they had found the most fun toy ever. The giant was clothed in rags, mostly, and the rags looked very old, like they had been weathered. Other children sat on the meadow and stared at her. The giant's head faced away. Firefly walked toward her, looking for some sign of life, a rising torso, perhaps, or a movement in the limbs, anything to indicate she was asleep. Firefly saw nothing.

The children stopped playing as soon as they saw Firefly. Cliff had stopped some distance from the giant. Firefly stood beside her. "She has so many tattoos," said Cliff.

"Yes," said Firefly. "I wonder why she is here."

Firefly did not want to go around to the other side to see the giant's face. She was afraid it would remind her of Mushroom's empty eyes. Instead she stood with Cliff and the other children. The presence of the giant here on this hill, in this meadow, was oddly comforting. It was as though this hill was not so foreign after all. Giants, or at least one giant, had been here before.

Firefly heard thundering feet behind her. She turned around. A group of grown ups advanced toward them. Her mother was part of the group. Firefly waved. The group, except for her mother, ran past her and descended on the giant. They went to the giant's feet and hands and used those easy access points from which to climb up on her. Firefly's mother stopped and put her hand on Firefly's shoulder.

"They don't look like your tattoos," said Firefly.

"No," said her mother. "It doesn't look like the work of any inker I know. It's very primitive. Almost like whoever did it had never done inking before."

Firefly saw what she meant. The images were stick figures and did not display the skillful lines, or depth of shading that her mother or any of the other inkers were able to do. "What are they doing on her?" said Firefly.

"They want to know where she came from."

"Why?"

"This place might be unsafe for us. They need to know if she died from something here. Now help me get the children out of here."

Her mother began gathering up the kids in the

meadow. Firefly found Cliff and asked her to get the kids together. Cliff nodded silently and went to each boy and girl. Soon they all began gathering at the edge of the meadow. Some of the adults on the giant jumped down and advanced with considerable speed back to the forest.

"Where are you going?" said Firefly as they passed by.

"We aren't staying in a place that kills giants," said one of them and kept walking.

"Where will you go?" said Firefly to their receding backs. If they answered, Firefly did not hear them.

Her mother returned, trailing half a dozen kids. "I want you to take them back to the settlement area," she said to Firefly. "Their parents will be worried about them."

"The ones who still have parents," said Firefly.

Her mother nodded. "Yes, the ones who still do."

"What are you going to do here?" asked Firefly.

"We need to find out more about this giant."

"What can you find out?" said Firefly. "She's dead."

"Giants don't die often, honey. We need to know what happened to this one."

Firefly looked at the people on the giant. They

moved over her like flies on a dead bird, something Firefly felt in her bones they should not be doing.

"I'll go back," said Firefly.

"I'll be along in a minute," said her mother. She turned from Firefly and returned to the giant.

"Come on kids," said Firefly. Cliff and the rest of the children gathered around her. Firefly put out her hands. They all held hands and walked back to the forest.

At the clearing things were already looking better. Some tents were up. Some people busied themselves by skinning dead dear, preparing the animals for cooking. Mr. Epiderm lay under a tent with a hastily constructed blanket of tree bark spread over him. The children scattered from Firefly and went looking for their parents or a place to play.

"I heard there's a dead giant," said Mr. Epiderm.

Firefly nodded. "She has tattoos but not like ours."

"A dead giant is a hard thing," said Mr. Epiderm. "They live so long. When one dies it is like losing a whole world. The other giants are going to be demoralized by this."

"I don't think this giant is one of them," said Firefly.

"Even so," said Mr. Epiderm, "just the sight or thought of such a thing. It is difficult."

"Where do you think she came from?"

"Impossible to say," said Mr. Epiderm.

A man brought a raw piece of the deer to Mr. Epiderm. "It won't be cooked for a while," said the man. "Thought you might like this little piece to tide you over."

"Thank you," said Mr. Epiderm. The man nodded and went back to the butchering.

Mr. Epiderm took a bite. He offered some to Firefly. She refused. She never liked raw meat, even though she did not think the raw fish she had earlier was so bad. Some river people who ate their deer raw said it retained the vital power of the animal. Firefly wasn't sure this was true, and her mother certainly never wanted her to eat raw meat.

"Oh," said Mr. Epiderm. "That *is* good. I am so hungry. You must be too."

"I am," said Firefly, "but I can wait."

Mr. Epiderm took several more bites and finished off the meat. His mouth was bloody. He looked strange, like an image from a dream. Firefly didn't like it. Mr. Epiderm licked his fingers and put his hand on his belly. "It is hard to be here like this, without any of our civilization to support us."

"Yes," said Firefly. "But what about the giant?"

"Ah," said Mr. Epiderm. "The giant, yes. I suspect she is one of the river people who went up the plateau to escape the gorge. It probably happened a long time ago. Remember, you were saying how river people could get away and survive on their own. I suspect you are right. Some did. But they did not live among the giants. They found their own way. I have heard stories and rumors of such things. It appears the stories might be right."

Firefly considered this. "Then why was she coming back?"

Mr. Epiderm shrugged. "Maybe she knew she was dying. She might have been on her way back to the gorge, to die near her home. She might have stopped here on purpose, within sight of the gorge, or she might have simply expired here by accident. Who knows."

Expired here. The phrase sounded so odd in Firefly's ear, as though Mr. Epiderm was reading from some strange sheet of his paper made from reeds.

"Tell me," said Mr. Epiderm, "is her skin intact?"

"I think so."

"I thought as much. The giants have such tough hides, you know. I have always thought that even in death their skin would be too touch to rot. Even the crows could not break through, isn't it so?"

"Yes," said Firefly. "It looks that way. Mom's trying to find out what killed her."

Mr. Epiderm nodded. "That would be a valuable thing to know."

"Do you think we ever lived up here?" said Firefly. "I mean, the people who were our ancestors?"

"I think our people did live in the mountains," said Mr. Epiderm. "The dead people in the river are proof of that. They were frozen in the glacier."

"How would they get in the glacier?"

"After they died they would get covered in snow over the seasons, which would eventually turn into a glacier."

"That would have taken many lifetimes," said Firefly.

Mr. Epiderm nodded. "More than we can imagine, probably. They may have been trapped for centuries. Eventually it probably got too cold for the pocket people still alive to remain and they came down to the gorge, but their dead remained in the glacier. When the volcano became active again, it began melting the glacier, releasing the dead people who had been trapped. All those tremors we've been feeling the last few weeks was the mountain waking up. I didn't recognize it until it was too late."

Firefly tried to wrap her mind around the idea of her ancestors frozen in ice. Who could even imagine a life from so long ago? "I don't understand," said Firefly. "I always thought we had been in the gorge forever, and now I find out that isn't true at all."

Mr. Epiderm looked past Firefly to the forest below them. The tops of trees stood like they could brush the sky. "When I was a young man," he said, "I thought the only thing that mattered in the world was inking. All I wanted was to put my pictures on the skins of the giants. When I grew up, that was exactly what I did. In those days the giants wanted tattoos more than anything. They had a desperation in them that required more and more pictures all the time. In Craddleton alone, we had at least twenty inkers and we worked most days. Then the demand began to diminish. Yesterday, in all the gorge, we had not much more than half a dozen inkers and none of them worked full time."

"You're saying things change," said Firefly.

"Things change," said Mr. Epiderm. "Yes. Maybe the giants will want tattoos again, but will there be river people to do it? Will your mother care about inking anymore? Will you want tattoos?"

Two days ago she wanted nothing more than to ink tattoos on giants. Now that she was to be giant, would she want to be inked? Who knew? She saw what Mr. Epiderm was saying. Inking didn't matter anymore. Their world was gone and inking would not bring any of it back.

Cliff and Bridge and several of the other children were playing a game. They ran around a tree, hiding from each other, filling the air with laughter and their footsteps, striking delicately on the ground in a resonant patter. The world had come to an end, but these children did not know any better. They still thought the world was an adventure. They still thought finding a dead giant was an occasion for merriment. They had minds that would be comforted by a song about breaking the bones of a giant.

"I don't think I care about inking anymore," said Firefly. "Maybe when I become a giant, I will want a tattoo. But I don't want to *ink* a tattoo. Not anymore."

"How different from even a day ago," said Mr. Epiderm.

"I know," said Firefly. "I always thought I would want to ink."

"Have you thought about your life when you become giant?" said Mr. Epiderm.

"No," said Firefly. "Should I?"

"I think it might pay you to consider it. Have you told your mother?"

"No."

"You need to do that," said Mr. Epiderm.

Firefly nodded. "But not yet," she said. "I still need to get used to it."

"Of course," said Mr. Epiderm. "I would not interfere. However, remember you are her only family. It will be hard for her to think of you being so separate. Things will be more different now than they have ever been before."

That sounded like a joke. Firefly looked at Mr. Epiderm to see if he was being witty. She saw no glow or twinkle in his eyes. In fact, they were drawn. Mr. Epiderm looked weary.

"What does that song mean?" she said.

"The song," said Mr. Epiderm. "I have pondered it myself many times. Inkers don't break bones, do they? But the song says we want to. I think the song is so old, we might never know where its sentiments come from."

Firefly's mother approached them from the direction of the dead giant.

"Fern," said Mr. Epiderm. "What did you discover?"

She looked at Firefly, who noticed a strange expression in her eyes, like she was puzzled by something.

"She broke her leg," said Firefly's mother. "I guess she fell and couldn't get up. It must be why she died, alone up here, maybe unconscious from the fall. She has lots of tattoos on her, but none of them were done by any inker I know. She got them somewhere else. Except for one, maybe. Lots of them, a big long story. There's people on a vine on her back. The higher up the vine, the bigger the person is. It's like a pocket person growing as she goes up the vine."

Mr. Epiderm's face seemed to brighten, but he said nothing. Firefly thought she knew what he was thinking. The vines. It was what made people giant. Firefly was going to be a giant because she climbed the vines and got that sticky stuff on her.

"There's other scenes," said Firefly's mother. "She's on an island, somewhere. It's like she went out to sea and lived on an island. I guess. I don't know. We tell stories when we ink, but where did she ink? Where did she go?"

"I don't know, Mom," said Firefly.

"You said one of the tattoos might be from here," said Mr. Epiderm.

Firefly's mother nodded. "She has a tattoo on her ankle," she said. "It's the most peculiar thing. It's exactly like the one on Thunder's ankle. It's a tattoo of a firefly."

THUNDER

Thunder stepped closer to the hill. A dead giant was not a good thing. He tried to remember the last time a giant had died. He knew of no giant deaths since he became giant. From talking to the other giants he had learned that one of them had died about thirty years before that. And before *that* no one could remember. So they were rare occurrences. Also, giants did not usually come up here to the mountains.

He trudged higher until he was above the tops of most of the trees. He turned to look back at the gorge. The smoke was less dense than it had been. The volcano was still oozing lava, however. Thunder missed his cave. Where would the giants now live? They were not suited to a nomadic life, but it was possible they had no other choice. He turned from the gorge and continued walking. At the top of the hill the pocket people, occupied with setting up their homes, appeared completely industrious and happy. They were busily sewing tents, digging pits for cooking food, and herding their children to safety.

Several of the pocket people looked up at him. *Where is the dead giant?* he signed.

They pointed across the clearing to a dense thicket of woods.

Thank you, he signed.

He stepped carefully through the clearing, being wary to avoid any of their structures, which, to him, looked as though they might fall over at any time. They had charm but very little in the way of strength. It could get cold and windy up here. Their shelter might not be sufficient. It was fortunate this disaster happened in the spring. If it was still the dead of winter, they could probably look forward to an early death. But then, if it was winter, they probably would not have taken the pocket people up here at all. They most likely would have gone to the sea instead.

The trees were shorter here. He could look over them to a meadow on the other side. He stepped onto the meadow. Pocket people milled around a fallen giant. Thunder stopped to survey the scene. He did not want to step any further. The sight of the downed giant was disconcerting to him, as though he was looking at his own death.

The pocket people on the dead giant stopped

and looked up at him. One of them signed to him. *Do you know this giant?*

Thunder didn't answer. He felt as though he wanted to step on all of them. What were they doing on this poor dead person? Doing what they do, which is trying to puzzle things out. Always digging, doing things, fussing at the controls of the world. He supposed they needed to see why this particular giant was dead. Thunder understood. He wanted to know himself. But surely they could go about it with a little more respect, couldn't they?

Maybe not. He stepped forward. The pocket people scattered. They moved to the edge of the meadow. Some of them put their hands over their chests and bowed their heads. Others did the same, then more and more. Finally they all stood in a row around the perimeter of the meadow and did not move.

Thunder came closer to the dead giant. She was covered in tattoos, but they were not like the ones he had seen on his neighbors. They were much more sophisticated, with a simple line and a style suggesting an artistry he had not seen from any of the inkers who had ever decorated him or any of his neighbors. Those tattoos were often elaborate affairs with many bright colors and intricate patterns, detailed images with lots of parts that were more like intricate paintings than mere tattoos.

The tattoos on this fallen giant, on the other hand, were spare renderings. A line here, a tiny squirm of ink there. The merest hint of detail in the outline. Her back displayed a large tattoo of vines, many strands of them, snaking from her neck down her spine. The vines were not detailed in any way, but they had figures on them in various sizes. People climbing the vines, as Leaf and Thunder had done so many years ago. These tattoos of the vines were like the trails certain insects leave on the ground: a simple record of where they had been.

There was more: Scenes of a giant on an island in the sea. Was this her life? Had she been to sea and come back here to tell them about it? He had no way to know for sure, but perhaps so. But on the way, it looked like she fell and broke her leg. That must be how she died.

Thunder looked at more of her tattoos, and saw something familiar on her broken lower leg, just above her ankle. Was it? How could it be?

Thunder moved close and fell to his knees. A shiver chilled him. There was no doubt. He had done this tattoo. It was different now: bigger, and stretched to a slightly faded blur. Which made sense, because when he had inked that tattoo on his sister, Leaf, he was only twelve. Leaf was fourteen. They had always liked fireflies and spent much of their time searching for them and capturing them. He inked an image of a firefly on her ankle. He had done it mere months before she left them forever.

So this dead giant was his sister.

Thunder felt as though his world had opened up under him. First Mushroom, now Leaf. How much death could one place harbor before it became all one would remember of it?

An awareness of the assembled pocket people came to him. They were all standing with their mouths open. He knew what this was. They were singing a long note. Periodically they took breaths, but they kept singing, their mouths open wide, pushing out their breaths. While they sang, they also signed. Thunder could hardly tell what they were signing at first. His eyes were welling up with tears and they all looked blurry and indistinct, as though they were old tattoos themselves, falling into indistinction from wrinkled old age.

He wiped his cheeks of moisture and studied their signing. They were all signing that song, the lullaby he remembered from when he was a boy, the one he had asked Fern about when he first brought her up on the plateau.

In morning light,
my heart's delight,

*is slinking in
and inking skin.*

*To draw the fire
of your heart's desire;*

*to break your bones
and hear your moans.*

They signed another verse:

*Our mourning starts
with hurting hearts,*

*we feel the moans
and hold our bones.*

*The life we draw,
the world we saw,*

*is sinking in
to soothe the din.*

Thunder did not know this second verse. The pocket people continued to sing and they kept signing, repeating the first verse, then the second, then going back to the first and so on.

So much feeling in those words. Did the pocket people truly believe tattoos were made to heal? Was that why he had wanted them for so long? And why had he stopped wanting them? Was it because Leaf died coming back to the gorge which was no longer there?

Thunder did not think about it anymore. He raised his hands to the sky, left them there for several seconds, then dropped them as rapidly as possible, and plowed into the earth. He pulled up clumps of sod, dirt, and rock and moved them over to the side. He put his hands into the dirt again.

He was an earth mover.

A planet changer.

He made a cradle for his sister.

He dug a long narrow trench beside her. As he worked, other giants came. They sunk to their knees beside him and began excavating the ground with him.

Moon arrived and put her hand on his back. Thunder, occupied by his task, ignored her. She put her other hand on his shoulder and pulled him back from his digging.

Are you ok? signed Moon.

My sister, signed Thunder. *She died here.*

Moon nodded. She looked sympathetic, like she wanted to make him feel better. *I remember Leaf,* she said. *I haven't seen her in a long time. How did she die?*

What does it matter? signed Thunder.

It might be good to know where she came from. How she got here.

I'm tired. Let me bury her.

Have you examined her tattoos?

What?

Her tattoos. Did you look at them.

What did it matter? *A little,* signed Thunder.

I think we should study them.

Thunder put his hands up on his head, like he had decided not to talk anymore.

I'll only be a minute, signed Moon. She stepped away from Thunder and approached Leaf. Thunder watched her. She did not have the proper sense of respect. At least none Thunder could see. Moon walked to the other side of Leaf and bent close to her. She examined the tattoos on Leaf's back. Thunder saw them from his vantage near the grave the giants were digging but could not make out the details. Moon stood up and motioned to him to come over.

Thunder hesitated. He did not see the point of this. He wanted only to put Leaf in the ground. Her continued presence above the earth, in this state, made him feel like he had failed her in some way.

The pocket people signed verse one. They signed

verse two, and went back to verse one.

Thunder, reluctantly and slowly, walked to the other side of Leaf and stood next to Moon. He made a point of avoiding Leaf's face. No need to see her in death.

Moon pointed to the tattoos on Leaf's back. Thunder forced himself to look, remembering Moon's back, the mini history of the giants and how they reconfigured the flow of the river. It had all been there. And now, here, on Leaf's back, another history. A lone giant, walking. Arriving at the sea. Walking into the water.

You see, signed Moon.

She lived at the ocean, signed Thunder.

Moon's eyes lit up. *Yes! She lived there. She prospered. We could do the same.*

What about the pocket people? signed Thunder.

They can come with us. We will take them. They will be happy on the beach.

Thunder struggled to come to terms with such a scheme. *We are not fish,* he signed.

Neither was Leaf. But she did it.

I don't know, signed Thunder.

I have always thought it a wonderful possibility, signed Moon. *We would not live in the ocean, of course. We would live on it. Near it. It would be the background to our lives.*

Thunder left Moon to her peculiar ideas and

went back to work with the other giants. They had almost dug a grave big enough for Leaf.

They all bent down. Thunder felt grief overwhelm him. He remained silent for a couple of minutes, then helped them finish digging the grave.

FIREFLY

"What does it mean?" said Firefly. "That the dead giant has a tattoo of a firefly?"

"Very simple," said her mother. "Your father once told me he and his sister loved fireflies. He had put a tattoo of a firefly on her ankle."

"So," said Firefly, "that dead giant is my father's sister? She's my aunt?"

Her mother nodded. "It appears so."

Firefly blinked. "What is she doing here?"

Mr. Epiderm spoke up. "She was separated from her tribe and was not able to survive on her own."

As he spoke the ground shook. Fern's father rose up from the forest and stepped onto the clearing. He was far enough away, at the other end of the meadow, that he did not notice them. Firefly raised her hand to him, but he had a brief conversation with several of the other river people. He moved on, toward the clearing across the copse of trees where the dead giant lay.

"He can't go there now," said Firefly's mother. "I have to go stop him."

Mr. Epiderm held her arm. "Are you sure you should go now?" he said. "He needs to find out eventually."

"Not like this," said Firefly's mother. "It's too hard. I need to tell him."

Firefly, who had been wanting to say something for a long time now, blurted out her news. "I'm going to be giant," she said.

Her mother stopped. "What?" she said.

Firefly instantly regretted saying anything. Especially now. She looked at Mr. Epiderm, who nodded his head, urging her to continue.

"My fingers hurt," said Firefly.

Her mother looked like she was going to faint. "Your fingers?"

"They're getting thicker."

"Let me see."

Fern extended her hands. Her mother took them and held them very tightly. Her eyes were wet. Her mouth tightened. "Oh no," she said. "Oh no, Firefly."

"I think it might be the vines." said Mr. Epiderm.

"The vines?" said Firefly's mother.

"Leaf's tattoos may have solved the mystery for

us. You said the figure grows as it climbs the vines. Well, there you are. Climbing those vines makes river people into giants."

"They have this stuff on them," said Firefly. "If you touch it, it burns you."

"When did you touch them?"

"When I climbed up looking for you. I never would have done it if I'd known. I don't want to be giant, Mom. I don't."

Firefly's mother looked like she was thinking back. "Thunder climbed those vines. He thought it was fun. I never did. I thought it was dangerous. Leaf must have climbed them too. But they're well hidden. How did you find them, Firefly?"

"Mushroom told me about them," said Firefly. "But he didn't know about turning into a giant. He said it was a way to get up top. To look for you."

"For me?" Firefly's mother shook her head. "Those vines should have been cut down a long time ago," she said. "They're dangerous. You can't become giant. You simply can't."

"No one knew what they would do," said Mr. Epiderm.

"I'm sorry," said Firefly. "I didn't mean it. I never wanted to be a giant. Never."

Her mother looked up at the sky and exhaled a deep long breath. "You'll live forever," she said. "Or so long it will seem forever."

"I know," said Firefly.

"I suppose I can be happy about that."

"Better that," said Mr. Epiderm, "than to let it depress you."

Firefly's mother nodded. "The vines are gone now, aren't they?"

"I expect so," said Mr. Epiderm. "Destroyed under the lava, I'm sure."

"That means my daughter will be the last giant."

"Yes," said Mr. Epiderm. "I suppose that's true."

Firefly heard the sound of many voices holding a long and eerie note. It sounded like someone was crying and feeling joy all at the same time. "What is that?" she said.

"People singing," said Mr. Epiderm. "It's coming from the direction of the dead giant."

"Does this have something to do with you turning giant?" said Firefly's mother.

"No, Mom. I don't know anything about it."

"It's an accompaniment," said Mr. Epiderm. "It's the sort of thing people used to hum with that lullaby."

Giants came up from the forest and walked toward the dead giant.

"Mr. Epiderm," said Firefly's mother, "is there any way to reverse the effect?"

"Reverse?" said Mr. Epiderm.

"I mean, can we keep Firefly from becoming giant?"

Mr. Epiderm shook his head. "I have never heard of such a thing," he said.

Firefly's mother slumped. "I don't have time for this, now," she said. "We need to go find your father."

She turned and began sprinting towards the clearing where Leaf had fallen. Firefly followed. They got to the clearing and found the giants already digging the grave. Firefly's mother ran toward Thunder. He looked her way. *What is it?* he signed.

Firefly could not tell what her mother signed in return. Firefly ran to be at her mother's side. She had seen the dead giant earlier, but now, knowing she was her aunt made her all the more imposing and sad.

Her mother signed some more things. Her father lifted his hands. He stopped and looked at her.

Firefly saw something in his eyes she had not seen before. Was it love? She couldn't be sure.

Is this true? he said. *You will be a giant?*

The river people still sang around her. They also sang the lullaby and another set of lines she had never heard before. Who knew that song had another verse?

Firefly held up her hands. *Yes.*

Her mother turned around. She had tears in her eyes.

Thunder stepped back. He ran into a giant who was standing next to Leaf's grave. The giant held Thunder and propped him up. Firefly pushed against the ground. She wanted to fly up to her father, but he was impossibly far away, living in the sky.

I have something important to do, he said. *We'll talk after.*

Firefly nodded.

Her mother signed to her father. *We wanted to be here. To say goodbye to her.*

OK, signed Thunder.

There's one more thing, signed Firefly.

Yes? signed Thunder.

If it is ok with you, I'd like to ink a tattoo on you.

Thunder blinked several times. His hands hung in the air, unable to form any words. Her mother looked at Firefly with surprise.

I was thinking a leaf, signed Firefly. *On your other leg. In memory of your sister.*

I would be honored, signed Thunder. *As long as your mother approves.*

Firefly half expected her to say no, just like she'd said no a million times before.

But she didn't.

I think it's a fine idea, signed her mother.

"Thanks Mom," said Firefly.

"I guess it's about time you got your wish," said her mother.

"Oh no," said Firefly. "I just realized we don't have any needles or ink. We left them all in Craddleton."

"We'll have to improvise," said her mother. "Go look for some berries in the woods. The juice will be our ink. I'll figure out how to make inking needles."

Firefly hesitated only a second, then bolted for the woods. She quickly found bushes of huckleberries in clear areas between groups of trees. She pulled off a couple of handfuls. They stained her palms purple.

She ran back to her mother, who had found some salmon bones from around the camp. She held up several of them for Firefly to see the pointed ends.

"Will they work?" said Firefly.

"They will have to. Come on."

Firefly's father was already stretched out on the grass, waiting patiently for his tattoo. Firefly and her mother walked up to his ankle.

"Do you know how to start?" asked her mother.

Firefly nodded. She took some of the huckleberries and smeared it on her father's ankle. She stood on tip toe to get high up on the skin.

"That's it," said her mother. "Spread the berries around."

Firefly's whole body felt alive, like she was about to burst with excitement. She was inking a giant!

Her mother showed her how to push the sharp end of a fish bone into Thunder's skin. Firefly watched carefully. As the point went in and came out, some of the juice from the berries seeped into the wound.

"Now you," said her mother.

Firefly took one of the bones in her hand. She was doing this for her father. He needed help to get over his grief. The tattoo would be his reminder of his sister for the rest of his life.

Firefly's heart rattled in her chest. She pushed the bone into Thunder's skin. She had to push hard to make it puncture his tough hide. She pulled the bone out of the wound and pushed it back in at a spot just a fraction of an inch away. She continued like this for a while, painstakingly applying huckleberry juice to every hole she made and being careful to keep the leaf shape going.

"You're doing a good job," said her mother. "I'm proud of you."

Firefly's brow was wet with perspiration. "Thanks, Mom," she said.

"I'm going to go see how he's doing," said her mother. She disappeared around the other side of Thunder's foot. Firefly continued piercing her father's skin and applying her makeshift ink. Before long she had finished the design. She used her shirt to wipe away the excess huckleberry juice.

She stepped back.

She examined the tattoo very carefully. It wasn't half bad at all. It looked exactly like a real leaf.

Her first tattoo.

And probably her last. Soon her fingers would be too big and clumsy to hold any inking equipment.

She dropped the fish bone on the ground and went around Thunder's foot.

She saw her mother signing to her father.

Are you feeling any better? signed her mother.

A little, signed her father. *The tattoo will help. Thank you for letting her do it. It means a lot to me.*

It probably means even more to her. Promise me you will keep her safe. After she becomes giant. I don't want to lose her.

I promise, signed her father.

The chorus of river people stopped their singing and their signing. The silence in the air was so complete that Firefly thought she had lost her sense of hearing. Her mind expanded away from her to fill the world. She thought for the first time that it was a small world. Easy to navigate and understand.

She stepped forward and stood by her mother.

I hope you like my tattoo, she signed to her father.

I already do, he signed.

Her mother took Firefly's arm and held it so tightly it felt as though it was going to break.

Firefly put her hand on her mother's arm and patted it lightly. Her mother loosened her grip. A little.

They stepped back while Thunder shifted his position and slowly, laboriously, rose from the ground. He walked to his sister Leaf.

The giants lifted Leaf up with exquisite gentleness and laid her in the grave softly. They covered her with dirt one handful at a time.

thunder

Thunder stepped back from his sister's grave. The assembled pocket people held their circle around him. Night was falling. The smell of burning wood was sharp in the air. Thunder realized he had not slept in a long time.

He looked down. Firefly looked up at him.

I'm sorry about your sister, she signed. *About Aunt Leaf.*

Thank you, signed Thunder.

We're roasting some venison. If you'd like to come eat with us.

Thunder was tired. He was also hungry. *We generally don't eat dead animals*, he signed.

That's too bad, signed Firefly. *I like eating deer. Will I have to give it up?*

Thunder considered the question. *I don't think you* have *to, but I think you will probably* want *to.*

Fern stepped in. *She needs to keep up her strength*, she signed. *What can it hurt to eat a little bit of meat?*

The circle of pocket people dispersed. They returned to their tents, their makeshift homes. Thunder wanted to give them somewhere else to go, but for now, for tonight, this would have to do. *I suppose it would be fine,* signed Thunder.

Good, signed Fern. *Come on.*

As they neared the site of the cooking deer, the smell of the seared meat filled Thunder's nostrils and instantly made his mouth water. Fern pointed across to the opposite side of the clearing, where other giants sat cross legged. Thunder, walking carefully, went to join them. The pocket people sat down in rows facing them. Thunder wondered if giant and pocket people had ever done this before. He supposed not. They had separate lives, had lived in different worlds for a long time. Now, with so many of their numbers gone, it was a melancholy time, a time for coming together.

Mr. Epiderm struggled to stand on his bent crutches. He put up his hands and began signing. At the same time, he spoke. Thunder could not hear him, but supposed he was saying the same words he was signing.

It is, perhaps, much too late coming, but we want to say to all of you a sincere thank you for all you have done for us over the years. It appears our old lives are now finished, but you saved us from death and we wish to extend to you our most sincere thanks.

The pocket people all stood and raised their arms and pounded the air with their fists. They were shouting. What they were shouting, Thunder had no idea, but he could see they were full of energy and gratitude. Firefly jumped up and down. Other children did the same. Thunder appreciated the gesture, but still felt only grief. So much lost in one day. His family, the river, the plateau, everything. And so many of the pocket people, gone.

Thunder stood. The pocket people stood still. *Thank you,* he signed. *I have always known you feel gratitude toward us. I have always tried to do my best for you all. Yesterday my clumsiness caused the death of a child. For that I will always feel shame and grief. I will not even ask you for forgiveness, as that would be too much to expect. Instead, I will pledge to you right here and now, that I and all the giants will do whatever we can to help you begin your lives anew.*

He sat down. They all, giant and pocket people alike, dug into the roasting deer, arrayed in pits before them. Thunder had to agree it tasted very good. Now why had he kept himself from this food for so long?

Firefly walked over to him. He looked down at her. The light was fading. She was signing something at him. What was it? He strained to see.

Do you miss hearing?

Did he? Sometimes. He wanted to hear voices,

and birds, and water. All those things. But at the same time, it was wonderful to have such peacefulness in him at all times. It made him think the world could hold more than grief and loss.

You get used to it, he signed.
I think that scares me the most, signed Firefly.
Really? signed Thunder.
Plus, we have no place to live.
We'll get used to that, too.
I miss them all. I miss my village. I miss the river.

Thunder remembered his first few weeks and months as a giant. How he wanted only to be alone, since everyone else wanted him to be alone. Now, none of them could afford to do that. They had to find a way to live together, not in separate realms, connected by a cliff and some vines, but in the same realm, a shared space where they could all be themselves and support one another. There had to be a way for their two worlds to connect.

Thunder looked at Fern. She sat on the ground with her arms wrapped around her legs, and she watched her child signing to her father. Thunder saw only love in her eyes.

We all miss what we have lost, signed Thunder to Firefly.

A spark rose from the trees behind his daughter. Then another. Thunder recognized the wobbling paths of the sparks immediately. They were fireflies, lighting the night air like stars in the sky.

But life is not about loss, he signed. *It's always about new beginnings.*

About the Author

Mario Milosevic lives in the Columbia River Gorge, a land of high cliffs, active volcanoes, and landscapes carved by massive floods that occured thousands of yeas ago. The geography of his home served as the inspiration for *The Last Giant*. He began writing stories when he was twelve years old and has not stopped since. Learn more at mariowrites.com.

Made in the USA
Charleston, SC
08 February 2011